Our Last
CRUSADE
OR THE RISE OF A
New World

"We will retrieve Lady Sisbell within a week, and I will bring her back home. Then this will all be over."

Rin Vispose

Extraordinary astral mage who serves as both Alice's attendant and Astral Guard. Brilliant assassin skilled at using earth magic and the weapons hidden under her maid uniform.

"Rin, aren't you a little *too* close to Iska?"

Aliceliese Lou Nebulis IX

Second-eldest princess of the Nebulis Sovereignty. Following the Nebulis queen's injury during the Imperial invasion, she becomes the queen's proxy and faces off against the Zoa and the Hydra, who plan to usurp the throne.

Our Last Crusade or the Rise of a New World

"…Now, this may sound odd for me to say, but people are going to get the wrong idea from this picture."

"Don't struggle or it'll be out of focus."

Iska

Swordsman in Unit 907 and a former Saint Disciple. Returns home to the Empire in order to go after Sisbell, who has been captured as part of the Hydra's plot…

Our Last CRUSADE OR THE RISE OF A New World

CONTENTS

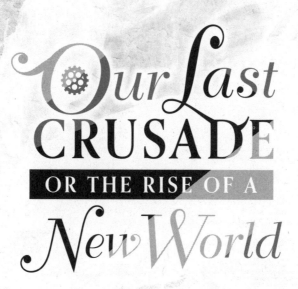

Our Last CRUSADE OR THE RISE OF A New World

9

KEI SAZANE

Illustration by
Ao Nekonabe

YEN ON

NEW YORK

9 KEI SAZANE

Translation by Jan Cash
Cover art by Ao Nekonabe

KIMI TO BOKU NO SAIGO NO SENJO, ARUIWA SEKAI GA HAJIMARU SEISEN Vol.9
©Kei Sazane, Ao Nekonabe 2020
First published in Japan in 2020 by KADOKAWA CORPORATION, Tokyo.
English translation rights arranged with KADOKAWA CORPORATION, Tokyo, through TUTTLE-MORI AGENCY, INC., Tokyo.

English translation © 2022 by Yen Press, LLC

Yen On
150 West 30th Street, 19th Floor
New York, NY 10001

Visit us at yenpress.com
facebook.com/yenpress
twitter.com/yenpress
yenpress.tumblr.com
instagram.com/yenpress

First Yen On Edition: June 2022
Edited by Yen On Editorial: Maya Deutsch
Designed by Yen Press Design: Liz Parlett

Yen On is an imprint of Yen Press, LLC.
The Yen On name and logo are trademarks of Yen Press, LLC.

Cataloging in Publication data is on file with the Library of Congress.

ISBNs: 978-1-9753-2214-4 (paperback)
       978-1-9753-2215-1 (ebook)

10 9 8 7 6 5 4 3 2 1

LSC-C

Printed in the United States of America

Our Last CRUSADE
OR THE RISE OF A
New World

Shie-la So hec jeek.
Please turn to me.

E r-nemne elma Ez suo lishe, r-harp riss phenoria uc Seo.
I blessed all you hold dear so you may grow.

Ris sia sohia, Ez xedelis fert Ez lihit siole.
I recalled what you truly desire.

THE HEAVENLY EMPIRE

Iska

Member of Unit 907—Special Defense for Humankind, Third Division. Used to be the youngest soldier who ever reached the highest rank in the military, the Saint Disciples. Stripped of his title for helping a witch break out of prison. Wields a black astral sword to intercept astral power and its white counterpart to reproduce the last attack obstructed by its pair. An honest swordsman fighting for peace.

Mismis Klass

The commander of Unit 907. Baby-faced and often mistaken for a child, but actually a legal adult. Klutzy but responsible. Trusts her subordinates. Became a witch after plunging into a vortex.

Jhin Syulargun

The sniper of Unit 907. Prides himself on his deadly aim. Can't seem to shake off Iska, since they trained under the same mentor. Cool and sarcastic, though he has a soft spot for his buddies.

Nene Alkastone

Chief mechanic of Unit 907. Weapon-making genius. Mastered operation of a satellite that releases armor-piercing shots from a high altitude. Thinks of Iska as her older brother. Wide-eyed and loveable.

Risya In Empire

Saint Disciple of the fifth seat. Genius-of-all-trades. A beautiful woman often seen in a suit and glasses with dark green frames. Likes Mismis, her former classmate.

THE NEBULIS SOVEREIGNTY

Aliceliese Lou Nebulis IX

Second-born princess of Nebulis. Leading candidate for the next queen. Strongest astral mage, who attacks with ice. Feared by the Empire as the Ice Calamity Witch. Hates all the backstabbing happening in the Sovereignty. Enraptured by fair fights against Iska, an enemy swordsman she met on the battlefield.

Rin Vispose

Alice's attendant. An astral mage controlling earth. Maid uniform conceals weapons for assassination. Skilled at deadly espionage. Hard to read her expressions, but has an inferiority complex about her chest.

Sisbell Lou Nebulis IX

Youngest princess of Nebulis. Aliceliese's little sister. Possesses Illumination, which reproduces footage of past events. Saved by Iska when she was captured in the Empire.

Lord Mask On

A member of the House of Zoa, which directly competes with the princesses for the throne. A conspirator whose true motives are unclear.

Kissing Zoa Nebulis

A powerful astral mage. Called the favorite child of the Zoa. Possesses astral power of thorns.

Salinger

Strongest sorcerer. Imprisoned for attempting to assassinate the queen. Currently at large.

Elletear Lou Nebulis IX

Eldest princess of Nebulis. Focused on traveling abroad. Often absent from the palace.

PROLOGUE

Welcome Home

"..."

Her wrists and ankles burned with pain. She tried to struggle, but it felt as though her whole body had been immobilized. The claustrophobic sensation and pressure brought Sisbell back to her senses.

"...Where is this place?"

Her throat was terribly sore, and her lips were dry, so she must have been out for a while.

"Where...am I...?"

She opened her eyes.

Sisbell Lou Nebulis IX was on her back. Thanks to the rusted shackles restraining her limbs, she could scarcely move.

The room was small, old, and filthy. The ceiling lamp likely had broken years ago, and the only light, if you could even call it that, came from between the slats of the wooden planks boarding the windows shut.

"............"

Cracks decorated the concrete walls, and the corners were filled with cobwebs. Though she couldn't catch a glimpse of the floor from where she was restrained on the bed, she was certain it would be carpeted by a thick layer of dust.

…*I cannot believe they would put me, a princess, in such a loathsome place.*

…*How utterly brazen.*

Things were slowly coming back to her.

She was sure she had been in the Sovereignty's central state right up until the moment she had lost consciousness. The Hydra, one of the royal families, had been keeping her captive in their stronghold when the witch Vichyssoise paid her a visit.

"I'll guarantee he'll live as long as you obey me. Your astral power is useful, after all."

"…What do you intend on making me do?"

"You'll find out once you wake up."

That was where her memories abruptly ended. And now she had come to.

Vichyssoise's disquieting proclamation was steadily taking a stranglehold over her chest.

…*While I was unconscious…*

…*they took me to a new location?*

What were the Hydra up to?

Apparently, they had designs on the Illumination astral power dwelling in Sisbell. Was that why she had been brought to this ominous room?

"…Is anyone there?! I'm sure you have surveillance cameras hidden somewhere in here! And that you can hear me!" she choked out while still lying faceup on the bed. The dust cloaking the room hurt her throat, but she paid it no mind. "If you'd like to win me over, you should at least prepare slightly better quarters for me. And take off these restraints!"

Then again, even if they had prepared a hotel room in the most luxurious establishment they could find, there was no way Sisbell would bow to the Hydra's whims.

"Are you listening?!"

"Oh my. Seems there's been a misunderstanding."

Creak…

The door opened, accompanied by the screech of rusted metal scraping against itself. A woman older than Sisbell entered.

"Nice to meet you. And welcome home," she said.

"…………"

"I suppose you're the shy type. You were screeching at the top of your lungs, but you went silent as soon as I arrived."

Sisbell saw dull red.

A woman with rouge hair that seemed as though it hadn't been combed in years had appeared. Her ashen skin suggested malnourishment, and the dark circles under her eyes betrayed her sleeplessness. She wore a washed-out white coat that made her seem like a doctor or researcher at first glance, but…

…Who is this lady?

…I've got a bad feeling about her. Just from the way she's looking down on me.

The woman's eyes were empty—the eyes of a passerby who had spied an empty can abandoned on the street and kept walking.

"…I have a lot of questions for you," said Sisbell, staring up at her. "You came here because you were responding to my request, yes? Then would you please enlighten me about what's going on?"

"Go right ahead. But whether I answer will depend on my mood," the woman replied.

"Where is this place?" Without pausing for a response, Sisbell continued. "Who are you? Why are you keeping me captive here? How long are you going to do that? …And most importantly, why did you say, 'Welcome home'?!"

"What an ambiguous query to start out with," the woman in the white coat murmured, sticking her hands into her black pants pockets. "If you mean you want to know the name of the country you're in, this is the Empire."

"...What did you say?!"

Anger overtook Sisbell before she could feel a rush of fear.

The Hydra, and Talisman, the head of the household—did that mean he had delivered her, a Sovereign princess, to the Empire of all places?!

"If you have questions about this facility, we will discuss them later," the woman continued.

"...We will?"

"It's relevant to your last question. And as for your second one about who I am, unfortunately, I don't intend to introduce myself."

Clack.

The woman's coat fluttered as she approached. She came right up to Sisbell's eye level, where the girl was restrained to the bed—no, even closer than that. Their faces practically touched as the woman bent down to behold her.

"A director of the Omen Institute for Astral Research...that's who I used to be."

"?"

"But I'm not anymore. Now I am Kelvina Sofita Elmos, independent female analyst. Oh, but I don't think there's really anything physically womanly about me."

They were nearly close enough for their noses to meet. Something brushed against Sisbell's chest.

"Eek?!" she cried out.

"What are you so surprised for? All I'm doing is examining you right now."

When Sisbell had felt the woman's fingertips—the fingertips of the researcher named Kelvina—groping her, she had screamed unintentionally.

"S-stop it! You brute…!"

"You really take after your sister."

"What?"

"Your astral crest's energy is exceedingly weak," Kelvina remarked. "I'd thought the Founder's descendants would all emit powerful astral energy, but it seems that doesn't apply to you or Elletear."

She righted herself.

The hands on Sisbell's chest—or, to be more accurate, on her astral crest—drew away and casually took their place back in Kelvina's pockets.

"To answer your third question, you're here as a research sample. I'm not sure how long you'll be staying. Until I'm satisfied, if I was to venture a guess."

"…………"

Sisbell was speechless.

More than the shame of her chest being groped or of being treated as though she were an object of research, it was the name Kelvina had invoked that truly horrified Sisbell.

Elletear.

Why had this strange woman mentioned the Lou family's first princess?

"This is the Birthplace of Witches. I understand you've seen Vichyssoise. She was the one who brought you here."

"…Witches?"

That was the derogatory term the Empire used for astral mages. Technically speaking, Sisbell was also a witch, and most of the citizens living in the Nebulis Sovereignty fell under this category. However…what Kelvina meant by *witches* was something else entirely—an astral mage who had given up their humanity. In other words, the stuff of fables—a monster and harbinger of disaster.

…*The Birthplace of Witches.*

5

...It can't be. Then that's how Vichyssoise ended up looking like that?

Had she been the result of barbaric human experimentation? And had that taken place in the Empire?

"Vichyssoise turned out well," Kelvina continued. "She was the first stable subject we created here."

"At the hands of the Imperials?!"

Her rage far outstripped her fear of being held captive.

"You treat we astral mages like witches yet create monsters yourselves!"

"That applies to your sister as well."

"...........Huh?"

"Didn't hear me? Your sister Elletear was also here in Elza's Sarcophagus. Though I suppose the difference between you two is that her stay was voluntary. She traveled all the way here from the Sovereignty in order to undergo the operation to become a witch."

"............"

She didn't understand.

What?

What was this Imperial saying? The first princess of the Lou household, her sister Elletear, had willingly come to the Empire?

"L-lies!"

"Believe me or don't believe me." Kelvina scratched her disheveled red hair and smiled wanly. "Your sister was magnificent."

Then she gazed up at the dim ceiling, staring into thin air, as though she was recalling the past.

"Normally, I have no interest in the human body, but she was the one exception," she said. "She was so captivating, sensual even. Her naked form was not that of a goddess. No, it was that of a demon, one who ensnares all men...and even *my* fingers trembled from the rush when I first laid eyes on her."

"...I don't want to hear any of that. I don't want to know about your tastes."

"But she made for a terrible specimen."

"What?!"

"She didn't have the level of obedience I desired. That's why I need an alternative. A purebred. If I was to describe my ideal, it would be someone from the same bloodline as her—"

Her white coat fluttered up. To the left and right of the researcher were rows of syringes containing faintly glowing agents.

"Yes, that's you, Third Princess Sisbell."

"What?!"

"That's why I said that before. 'Welcome home.' I'm sure I will be able to get quality antibody research out of someone from the same bloodline as her. Now, which injection would you prefer first?"

Imperial territory, ???. Elza's Sarcophagus.

The princess's scream rang out in the Birthplace of Witches.

CHAPTER 1

Out of the Paradise of Witches

1

The central state.

A hotel room in the heart of the metropolis. Close to the Nebulis palace.

"Huh? That's weird. Where did I put it again?" Nene asked. The Imperial Unit 907 member looked down at her wide-open suitcase and tilted her head quizzically.

Nene Alkastone. Her red hair, done up in a voluminous ponytail, and her large eyes left quite the impression. She wore a cheerful, friendly smile on her face. Though she was still only fifteen, her long, slender limbs gave her an air of maturity, like a model.

"No matter how many times I count them, I keep coming up one short...," she muttered.

"What's wrong, Nene? What have you been looking for?"

The female commander who approached her was Mismis. In contrast to Nene, an early bloomer, Mismis still looked like a teenager at twenty-two on account of her baby face.

"We have to leave soon," Mismis said. "We need to meet Miss Rin in the hotel lobby."

"Wait, Commander! Just give me a teensy-tiny bit longer to look for it!"

"What are you missing?"

"My towel." Nene's answer was a surprisingly homely item. "I can't find one of the towels I brought from the Empire."

"…Oh. Just that? You had me worried it was something important." Mismis broke out into a strained grin. "I was convinced you'd lost your underwear. Just like I have."

"Commander?! Wait, what did you just say?!"

"Oh, nothing. You shouldn't worry too much about it, Nene. What's so bad about leaving a towel at the hotel?"

"Hmm…," she hummed.

"Was it special?"

"Not really, but I made it myself. And I did a really good job on it, too, so it was one of my favorites." Nene folded her arms, looking uncomfortable. "I guess it's fine. I can just make a new one. I do wonder how much it'll burn, though."

"…How much it'll *burn*?" Mismis repeated.

"Yeah. With a blaze about this big." Nene pulled out a lighter, which produced a demure flame when she lit it. "If I do that, the towel should create a giant explosion. I brought it with me from the Empire 'cause it has enough force to blow the whole hotel lobby to smithereens. You know—for self-defense."

"That sounds more destructive than defensive, Nene!" Mismis exclaimed.

"I hope no one picked it up…"

"We need to find this thing now! It's an emergency!"

"But that's exactly what I haven't been able to do," Nene lamented.

Ding-dong. The doorbell of their suite rang.

"Hey, boss, Nene, we've gotta get to the lobby soon," said Jhin, the silver-haired sniper, as he appeared from the hallway. He carried a travel bag on his left shoulder and a golf bag concealing his sniper rifle on his right.

Jhin produced a towel.

"Also, we found this thing on the floor in Iska and my room. Is it yours, boss?"

"Uhhh!" Nene pointed to the item and cried out. "That's it! That's it! That's mine! Oh, when we had the meeting earlier, I must have—"

"What? It's yours? Looked kinda weird and beat-up, so I thought it was the boss's."

Jhin started to pass the towel to Nene...

...but instead headed over to the hallway.

"It's dirty, so I'm gonna toss it. This thing can go in the combustibles bin, right?"

"You can't burn iiiiiit!"

"Put it with the nonflammables!"

Nene and Mismis both scrambled to stop him.

First floor of the hotel. Front entrance.

A section of the lobby full of tourists and businessmen.

"...Sistia?"

Iska opened an eye and glanced over when he heard the soft footfalls behind him.

There, in a nook by a pillar that held the ceiling aloft...stood a brunette. Sistia, an astral mage with the astral power of Echo and servant to the House of Lou. She blinked, her eyes wide with surprise.

"...How did you know it was me? Weren't you turned away from me?"

"Your footsteps clued me in," Iska explained.

"Well. I was expecting you to say that, but I'm not the only servant from the House of Lou who might approach you, whether you could hear me or not. Why didn't you think it was Nami, Yumilecia, Ashe, or Noel?"

"Sure, but…" Iska simply gave a nonchalant shrug in response to her question, which anyone in her position would have asked. "We've been together at this hotel for nearly a week. I was bound to memorize your footsteps sooner or later, whether I wanted to or not."

"You mean you've committed the sound of all five of our strides to memory?"

"Not the sound so much as the rhythm. I wouldn't be able to tell if you started picking up the pace, though."

"Weirdo."

"…A little more positivity would be appreciated."

"As a servant of the House of Lou, I cannot go about praising an Imperial soldier."

She was truly unrelenting. Then again, this was probably how their relationship should be, since it was unheard of, nay, unprecedented for Imperial soldiers like them to be here in the Nebulis Sovereignty, the Paradise of Witches.

"So just to be clear, can you really afford to say 'Imperial soldier' out in the open?"

"I'm muffling our voices using my astral power, of course. Anyone more than two inches away from us wouldn't be able to hear a thing."

Her Echo astral power could draw in sounds. She had acted as their detector at the Hydra's astral power research institute, Snow and Sun, when they'd been searching for Sisbell.

"We have received a message from Lady Rin. Though preparations took some time, it seems that you will soon depart. The airplane has also been arranged, as anticipated."

"What about you?"

"We servants will go back to the safe house once you have left the hotel. It will take some time until the villa's reconstruction is complete."

"Got it."

"Please be more concerned for Lady Sisbell's safety than ours."

Next to Iska, the brunette quietly leaned against the giant pillar.

"Lady Sisbell was taken to Imperial territory. You are certain about that, correct?"

"That's all we can assume. It's our one and only clue."

According to Princess Mizerhyby, the Hydra had kidnapped Sisbell. That had been their goal from the start.

"Isn't this *what the sorcerer seeks?*

"Get it out of him, will you? And ask him how he knows of the Gregorian Descant."

Mizerhyby Hydra Nebulis IX, the next in line for head of household. Iska had successfully stolen one of her earrings.

...The Gregorian Descant, huh.

...I've never heard of it, and it seemed like Rin and Alice hadn't, either.

It was probably a Hydra code word. Though it most likely referred to a plot to overthrow the nation, their top priority at the moment was finding Sisbell.

"Please make sure you bring her back." Sistia lifted her head and stared, her intense gaze practically boring into him. "You told me this once: 'If I can't do it, you can take my life yourself.'"

"I'm not repeating myself," he replied.

"That won't be necessary. I only came here to confirm you did say it."

The brown-haired girl stood up, then heaved a long sigh, as though letting something off her chest.

"And please take care of Lady Rin."

"I don't think any of us have to worry about her."

"True enough. She's strong." Sistia forced out a laugh. "Lady

Rin is more than just a royal attendant; she holds multitudes. All I can ever accomplish are chores, but she's a member of the Astral Guard. She is one of the elite, further up than I could ever aspire to, and selected by Her Majesty herself. I should not have had any worries at all."

Sistia turned. She merged into the crowd of tourists walking down the hallway, her retreating back disappearing before long.

Iska was left alone.

"…Wonder if Commander Mismis and the others are done yet."

He shouldered the golf bag hiding his astral swords as he looked around.

2

The Nebulis palace. Otherwise known as the Planetary Stronghold.

Once, countless astral powers had gathered and crystallized to create the fortress. Ordinary flame could not harm the halls in the slightest. Even if a bomb was dropped on it, the palace would be able to reconstitute itself in but a single night.

And indeed, in the Star Spire, abode of the Lou family, there was not a single scratch to be found on the outer walls. Despite the blaze from the Imperial forces' bombardment, the walls were already fully restored.

"We need not worry about the royal palace! Though the queen has yet to heal, I will be sure to do a splendid job of supporting her!"

Star Spire.

In the Jewelry Box of Bells, the princess's private chambers, Alice placed her hand to her chest and resoundingly declared, "Now, Rin."

"…………" Her handmaiden was silent.

"Midday today, you will fly out of the Sovereignty. You will

do so for the sake of the House of Lou, the Sovereignty, and our futures. You must infiltrate the Empire!"

"...Haaah."

"I am counting on you, Rin. No one else would be able see such an important duty through! ...Wait, what's wrong? You look so very pale."

"...Does it seem that way? I suppose it does."

Rin was listless. Still looking pallid enough to faint, Alice's attendant, Rin Vispose, sighed. Incidentally, that had been her eighteenth of the day.

".......Lady Alice," Rin implored.

"What is it?" Alice asked.

"My family has served the royal family for generation after generation. My father and his father attended to the House of Lou in succession. And I have served you, the most likely candidate for the queen's successor, who people already see as the current monarch, since we were children."

"Yes, it's exactly as you say." Alice nodded without hesitation. "I am the person I am now because of you. I'm truly grateful for it."

"Yes. And so great was my desire to serve you that I labored as your attendant and dedicated myself to training in order to become your guard."

Each member of the Nebulis family had two attendants. One would serve as a handmaiden for their everyday activities. The other was a member of the Astral Guard, an escort who would protect the family member's life. Only astral mages who had undergone rigorous training and passed final exams personally administered by the head of the family could be appointed as one.

Rin had accomplished both roles all on her own. In this regard, she was unique, an exception. Among all three families, the Lou, Zoa, and Hydra, Rin was the only servant who fulfilled both duties for her princess.

"I am happy if you are happy, Lady Alice," she said. "As long as I am by your side, I want for naught."

"Yes, we do have a very strong bond."

"However, if I may speak for myself?"

"Yes, Rin?"

"Why are you making me go to the *Empiiiire*?!" the maid shrieked, dressed in a dark suit she wore for outings. She would be heading to the Empire in it. "...Argh, I can't believe this."

"You're going to save Sisbell. You'll only need to endure it for a week at most."

"I'm fully aware of that, but..."

Rin's shoulders drooped. Alice grasped the hand of her unusually despondent attendant and nodded slightly.

"Don't be so glum. Look. You can keep this safe."

She placed an earring fashioned in the image of a sun in Rin's palm. It was the earring belonging to Princess Mizerhyby of the Hydra, which Iska had stolen at the astral power research center Snow and Sun. They had learned a peculiar IC card was housed within it.

"Iska said that the princess called this the Gregorian Descant, right?"

"Yes. And we think it's one of the Hydra's secrets. It has strong encryption on it, so we'll need specialists to decrypt it into readable text. The only information we could view was..."

"Where they're taking Sisbell. That's why I'm leaving it with you."

She was outside of the Sovereignty. Sisbell, the third Lou princess, had been taken to the Empire. It was entirely plausible the Hydra and the Imperial forces were connected.

...The Empire wants a purebred, after all.

...Could the Hydra be looking for a ransom from the Empire in exchange for Sisbell?

And this did not stop at her sister. Two others were missing following the aftermath of the Imperial forces' invasion of the palace:

—House of Lou, Eldest Princess Elletear.

—Head of the Zoa, Growley.

There was no mistaking it. In all likelihood, the two of them had been taken to the Empire just like Sisbell.

"It's imperative that we turn things around. I need you to internalize that, Rin."

"I am deeply aware." Rin scowled. "We should be able to uncover the culprits behind the palace invasion using Lady Sisbell's Illumination astral power. You can rest assured that I'll get her out of there. Especially since we need her…to expose the Hydra's schemes, too."

Rin turned around and faced a girl who had been watching her exchange with Alice from a corner of the living room.

"I am counting on you to stay by Lady Alice's side while I am away," Rin told her.

"Y-yes, ma'am…!"

She was around Sisbell's age.

The petite girl's face still held the remnants of childhood, and her black hair had been cropped to her shoulders. Faint gray light from an astral crest, proof of her status as an astral mage, glowed on the nape of her neck.

She possessed the Silhouette subspecies of astral crest, which could create doppelgängers.

"I have orders from Her Majesty. As soon as you leave Lady Alice's side, Miss Rin, the Zoa and Hydra will take note. They'll probably suspect something."

"I estimate they'll catch on in about a week. Though I am sure that keeping up your astral powers for that long will tire you out."

"N-not at all! I'll put everything I've got into this…!"

The young girl bowed. At the same instant, sparks popped. Her form began to unravel like a thread as another girl materialized in her place—a girl with brown hair and sharp features wearing a housekeeping uniform—another Rin.

"Lady Alice," she said in *Rin's* voice. "Rin Vispose, this is what I have to offer… Is it to your liking?"

"It will work splendidly." Alice gave a firm nod to the girl who had disguised herself as Rin. "Your voice has a slightly different intonation, but I am sure no one will notice such a subtle distinction. This will work for a week."

This girl was the Lou's special secretary. Despite her youth, she was the royal family's first choice when they needed a body double. Typically, however, she acted as the substitute for the queen—this time she would be entrusted with covertly filling in for Rin.

"What do you think, Rin? Since this is you, after all."

"…………"

The Rin wearing the suit stared at the Rin in the housekeeping uniform. The genuine article looked over the other girl from head to toe several times.

"I see no issues. But if I must comment on something, I believe the real me has slightly higher shoulders, a more striking nose, and, of course, a slightly larger chest."

"…Uh, um," the girl masquerading as the attendant stammered, incredibly hesitant. She turned her face down. "My astral powers reproduce the form of others…so my features and build are exactly the same as yours, Miss Rin."

"…"

"S-so…that is to say, if you're concerned about my chest, then…"

"Uh-uh! Stop right there!"

What in the world is she doing? Predicting what the doppelgänger was about to say next, Alice called out to stop her.

"Enough talk of bosoms!" the princess exclaimed. "Please refrain from wounding Rin's pride any further!"

"What do you mean by that, Lady Alice?!"

"I'm already putting her through enough distress sending her to the Empire as is! I won't stand for her to suffer more on top of that! Please pretend that Rin's bust is bigger than yours!"

"Don't you see how that'll hurt my feelings even more?!" her servant exclaimed. "I didn't ask you to do that!"

"There, there," Alice said. She took the hand of her red-faced attendant in a parting handshake. "When you return from the Empire, I hope that the experience of overcoming such a terrible mission will have brought you growth in both body and mind. Especially in the chest."

"I find that absolutely unnecessary!" Rin cradled her suitcase in her arms as she ran out of the princess's room. "But fine, then! In that case, I'll make sure I come back even more well-endowed than you, Lady Alice!"

3

Nebulis Sovereignty. Fourth State Zahlfahlen.

Zahl International Airport. Closest airport to the central state.

"All right. I tried to keep my morale up in front of Lady Alice, but now that we're about to board the plane, I feel so down...," murmured Rin gravely.

"Huh? What's wrong? Why did you stop all of a sudden?" Iska abruptly whipped around.

Rin was in her perfectly pressed suit with her luggage in hand. She looked like a businesswoman heading out on a work trip in another country.

"We're supposed to keep from arousing suspicions in the airport. You were the one who told us that, Rin."

"......Iska."

Rin glared at him bitterly. The only reason she hadn't called him *Imperial swordsman*, her usual address for him, was because they were in a Sovereign airport. They couldn't risk anyone overhearing.

"There's no way you could understand how I feel. How could you possibly comprehend the agony of leaving Lady Alice's side, along with the grief of being forced to set foot in the vile territory of an enemy nation?!"

"I—I guess I don't, but…"

The long and short of it was that she didn't want to go to the Empire. Although it was Iska's birthplace, Rin saw it as both a malevolent superpower and the pioneer of the derogatory terms *witch* and *sorcerer*, which referred to astral mages.

"So now you see."

Rin began to walk off unsteadily. She wasn't heading to the plane's boarding gate but rather to the shopping area behind it.

"At the very least, I shall buy reminders of my motherland… souvenirs from the Sovereignty. Oh, they have Sovereign cookies with faces of past queens on them. I was always dubious about who would possibly want to purchase these things, but now even they feel nostalgic to me. I suppose I'll get one."

"But, um, Rin."

"What?"

"We're heading to the Empire. If you bring Sovereign cookies there, I'm pretty sure you'll look fishy."

"…………" She stopped in her tracks. Still clutching the small box of cookies, she felt her shoulders start to quiver. On top of that, her face turned red. "Stupid!"

"Whoa?! Wait, Rin, throwing souvenir boxes around is rude!"

"Shut up! Shut up! You should just be grateful that these weren't knives!"

Iska caught the boxes she'd hurled, then snuck them back onto the display shelf, trying to avoid being seen by the shop employees.

"Besides, it won't be a long trip," he reminded her.

"...Obviously. As if I could stand being in the Empire for two whole weeks or, God forbid, three."

It seemed she had finally accepted it. Her breathing was steady as she continued into the airport.

That was when Commander Mismis made it to them as well. Nene and Jhin were behind her.

"Oh, there you are! Iska, Miss Rin, please hurry," Mismis said. "It looks like boarding has already started, and the airplane is about to take off!"

"There's no need to panic," Rin replied flatly. "It's right after the baggage inspection."

"But the inspection line goes on forever! Just look over there," Nene said. "All the other economy customers are in a huge queue!"

"That's not where we're going. It's farther back."

Rin opened an employee-only door and headed inside. Or so it seemed...

Once they passed through the entrance, they came upon a corridor without a single worker in sight.

"It's a passageway for the royal family," Rin explained. "We can go right past the baggage inspection to the boarding gate. This hallway is specifically used by the Lou family, so we need not fear the Zoa or Hydra seeing us."

"What?!"

"That's unfair!"

"There's nothing untoward about it. If we went through the regular line, there's no way we would be able to pass through the baggage inspection. We'd cause a huge scene merely brushing up against the metal detector."

Rin's suit jacket was lined with sharp knives, and her business-card case held thin, needlelike assassination tools.

"Obviously. Otherwise, I'd never have been able to carry my guns onto the plane." Jhin nodded, shouldering his golf bag.

"I guess that applies to my firearms, and the commander's, too," Nene said. "And Iska's swords."

"...But this isn't all good." Rin looked straight ahead as she walked down the deserted hallway. "Lady Sisbell must have been abducted using this same method. Surely her captors boarded a plane using the royal passageway as brazenly as we are now."

She removed from her pocket an earring crafted in the image of a sun. If they were to trust the confidential files Princess Mizerhyby had called the Gregorian Descant—and the supposed intel about Sisbell's whereabouts was to be believed—Sisbell was already in the Empire.

"Iska." Rin, who was in front of everyone else, turned to look at him. "The world treaty has provisions detailing the humane treatment of prisoners. Torture and human experimentation are forbidden. Both the Sovereignty and the Empire have ratified the document. Is that correct?"

"...It is."

Inhumane treatment was indeed forbidden. Every nation without exception had agreed upon the clauses Rin had mentioned.

...*At least for appearances.*

...*They only agreed for political reasons, so the other countries wouldn't condemn them.*

But behind the scenes?

The Empire conducting experiments on captured witches. The Sovereignty enslaving detained Imperial soldiers. Both seemed plausible, but he honestly didn't know whether either was really going on.

Unit 907 was merely a collection of foot soldiers in the much larger entity known as the Empire. Whether they liked it or not, the number of secrets that were kept from them overwhelmingly outweighed the ones they were privy to.

"I'm sure you won't like me saying this, but I'll still put it out there anyway: I don't believe the Empire would honor stipulations requiring them to treat their prisoners humanely."

"............"

"Because the Sovereignty doesn't, either." Rin could say that now because the lady she served wasn't present at the moment. "The reigning sovereign has been called a moderate comparatively, but as for the rest of the royal family... Well, you've seen the Hydra. They're the types who would dare to plot the queen's assassination if they had to. They'll dirty their hands by whatever means necessary to achieve their goals."

"Even when it involves Sisbell?"

"That's exactly what I am saying. We'll be too late if they do something to her."

That was why they were hurrying. They didn't have the time to travel by car or by train from the Sovereignty to Imperial territory, which would have taken several days.

Torture, human experimentation...

They could not fathom what the Empire and the Hydra family would do with a Founder's descendant, one of the best witch samples they could hope for.

"The battle will be brief but decisive."

The sun earring disappeared back into Rin's pocket.

Then she declared firmly, "We will retrieve Lady Sisbell within a week, and I will bring her back home. Then this will all be over."

However...

Her sojourn in the Empire would not last a week as expected.

Neither Iska nor Rin knew the future that awaited them—a future tied to the discord that would envelop the world.

CHAPTER 2

Homecoming and Home Call

1

Nebulis Sovereignty. Star Spire.

The sharp cracking of earthenware resounded within Alice's study.

"Oh?"

She turned to identify the source of the sound.

Alice saw a broken teacup and Rin, who was gathering its shattered fragments.

"I will get this cleaned up right away," she told Alice, solemnly collecting the shards.

"Don't worry about it. I know it's your first time working as a housekeeper."

"...I'm terribly sorry."

She spoke with Rin's voice. The girl using her astral power to disguise herself as Alice's attendant gave the princess a small bow. She wasn't used to this.

Until now, she had served as a body double, acting as though she were the most important members of the royal family. She had transformed herself into eminent people like queens and ministers in the past. As far as Alice could tell, the girl was most familiar with taking up these stately roles.

This was the first time she'd played the part of servant, so she wasn't used to waiting on nobles. The mishap that had resulted from Alice asking for tea was a prime example of that.

…I'm impressed that she hasn't broken character even after making a mistake.

…But I suppose the disguise really is only skin-deep, huh.

As an attendant, Rin embodied perfection. Even if Alice hadn't known the circumstances, she would have doubtlessly realized the girl was a fake from witnessing this single mistake.

"How old are you again?" Alice asked.

"I am sixteen. And I will be seventeen this year," the girl replied.

"Oh, I'm sorry," Alice said. "I didn't mean you as Rin but your actual age."

"I'm fifteen."

She was still school-age. Her true identity was that of a tender black-haired girl, and one who gave off an air of timidity at that—a far cry from the Rin she was now.

…She must push herself to act like a grown-up while on the job.

…I'm honestly impressed, but…

Her guise wouldn't pass muster against wily military veterans. Lord Mask of the House of Zoa or Talisman, the head of the House of Hydra, would realize something was off with only a glance.

"The conference is in the afternoon—is that right?"

"Yes. It starts at one."

They were holding meetings on a daily basis now. Imperial forces had invaded the Sovereignty's borders and launched an attack on the palace. The government had yet to decide what retribution they would pursue on behalf of the many who'd been wounded and the royal family members who'd been abducted.

At the moment, the ruling families had come into a three-way conflict of opinion:

The Lou insisted they should rally around the queen to restore the country.

The Zoa insisted they should launch an all-out war with the Empire.

The Hydra insisted they were in need of a new queen and that the conclave was necessary.

Alice couldn't give in to them. The Zoa would not shy away from making casualties of their own citizens in a full-blown conflict between the Empire and the Sovereignty, while the Hydra were the very criminals who had attempted to overthrow the government.

"I will represent the Lou family as the queen's proxy," said Alice. "I gather Lord Mask and Lord Talisman will be in attendance, yes?"

"......Um, Lady Alice." The girl, who had finished cleaning the floor, looked apologetic. "Would it be possible for me to wait here?"

"............"

She was smart.

If the girl was in the same space as Lord Mask and Talisman, they would realize from her clumsy mannerisms that she was a body double. She must have proposed this after realizing that was on the princess's mind.

"Let's go together." Alice gave the girl a light pat on the back and a determined smile. "If Rin isn't there like she usually is, they're *more* likely to think something is off, right?"

"...B-but..."

"The real Rin would never be so faint of heart."

"Oh!"

"Have some confidence. Your astral power is splendid, so you can present yourself out in the open without fear."

"Y-yes, Lady Alice!"

The girl pretending to be Rin nodded firmly. As she smiled back, Alice glanced at the clock on the wall. The plane should be arriving now.

Soon, Rin would be in the Empire.

"...Iska wouldn't break our promise. Please trust him, Rin."

"Iska?"

"N-no, nothing!"

When the keen-eared attendant questioned her, Alice gave a flustered wave of her hands, as though shooing her away.

2

Opuhna. Independent state.

Sandwiched between the Empire and the Nebulis Sovereignty were several autonomous nations. Among them was Opuhna, a country along the easternmost edge of the Empire.

It was a nexus, so to speak. No air route directly connected the Nebulis Sovereignty and the Empire. Planes would instead stop at Opuhna, which was independent. Past that, you had to take the highways stretching across the continent and enter the Empire via vehicle.

"...It's already right in front of us."

The road stretched into the horizon. Iska gazed ahead from the passenger seat of the large car as he glanced at the map in his hands. Soon, they would probably come across an Imperial checkpoint on the highway they were racing down. If they could get through without incident, they would be in the Empire.

"Commander Mismis." He addressed the woman sitting in the back seat. "We're almost at the Imperial border checkpoint. All we have to do is show them our Imperial certificate of registration and Imperial force IDs, right?"

"Yeah, I don't think we need to hide who we are. We're just heading home, after all." Commander Mismis nodded, an Imperial-grade high-voltage stun gun resting on her lap.

Anyone from another country in possession of such a weapon would raise suspicion at a border checkpoint, but an Imperial soldier carrying one for self-defense was sure to be accepted. Even Jhin's rifle, which had been disguised as a hunting gun, could be carried into the Empire openly without issue. The same held true for Iska's astral swords.

"When we crossed the Sovereign border, I feared for my life, but we can relax now that we're going through the Imperial border checkpoint," Jhin said, as though remembering. "We have some stuff to deal with when we get back to the Empire, but all we're doing is coming home. We can just pretend we got back from sightseeing. The only part of this that might make for a recipe for disaster, though, is…"

He glanced over. Out of the corner of his eye was Rin, sitting directly beside him at the very edge of the back seat. She was the only one the conversation didn't apply to. At the moment, she was engrossed in reading a tourist guide on the Empire.

"…I see. So this is an Imperial note. It looks exactly like it did in history class." She held a bill from the Sovereignty in her left hand. Then she unfurled a note from the Empire in her right hand and compared them. "Mm-hmm. Apparently, you can use any common world currency in the Empire, but ninety-seven percent of the citizens opt for Imperial notes. If I use the common notes, they'll suspect I'm from abroad. Even if I make it into the Empire, if they find out I'm from the Sovereignty, everything will be for naught…so I'll have to use Imperial currency to remain innocuous…"

"It's all up to whether she can behave herself, I guess." Jhin gestured at Rin, who was still staring down at the guidebook. "It'll make things easier on us if she acts like a tourist. As an Imperial,

I don't know how to feel about getting a front-row view of a spy studying up to sneak into the Empire."

"Same here." Rin pouted and turned. Though she hadn't engaged in any of their conversations up until that point, she must have been listening in absentmindedly. "You all came to the Lou family's villa. The servants were terribly upset by that as well."

She was probably referring to the young women who served the Lou family: Yumilecia, Ashe, Noel, Sistia, and Nami. Despite their youth, they were all trusted retainers of the House of Lou.

And the strength of their loyalty was matched only by their hatred for the Empire.

"Imperial soldiers coming to the residence was unprecedented. Normally, the servants would have instantly handed you over to the military police, or at least mixed mud into your meals, or humiliated you by taking photos of you with hidden cameras while you were bathing. They discussed every trick in the book to upset you."

"Of course. We were expecting the room to be bugged."

"They would never." Rin shook her head tersely at Jhin. "Lady Sisbell kept a close eye on them. She called in each one of the five servants individually and admonished them, telling them that any slight against you would be taken as a slight against her."

"...She did?"

"It is as I said. I won't go as far as to press you to think of yourselves as being in her debt, but I hope you will remember what she did for you."

Rin crossed her arms. Or rather, she turned to her left as though she had recalled something herself. "Now, a change of subject, Commander Mismis."

"Y-yes?!"

"..."

Rin pointed at her left shoulder. When Commander Mismis saw that, she quickly placed her hand on her own left shoulder—to her glowing, greenish-blue astral crest. Of course, the light was currently masked by a self-adhesive.

"I'm sure you're wearing one of the Sovereignty's self-adhesives. How many days have you been using it?"

"...Um, about five."

"And what did you do when you bathed?"

"...I think I might have left it on."

"You should change that before we reach the Imperial checkpoint, just in case. If the self-adhesive deteriorates and any amount of astral energy leaks out, you'll be the one they capture."

"Y-yes, ma'am!"

"And while I'm at it, I think this one would match your skin more closely."

Rin produced a self-adhesive from her breast pocket. As far as Iska could tell, it looked the same as what Commander Mismis already had on.

"I'm sure you're using one of the self-adhesives Lady Sisbell had on her person, but her skin has not seen the light of day. Yours is different from hers."

Sisbell's skin was as white and clear as porcelain.

But that wasn't the case with Mismis. What Rin had meant to say was that Mismis needed a self-adhesive that would reflect the regular sun exposure she received during the Imperial forces' training sessions.

"This is one of mine. It should suit you better."

"Th-thank you, Miss Rin!"

"If you're caught, then everything will be for naught. That's all there is to it."

She was curt. Though being matter-of-fact was typical for Rin...

"............"

"What is it, Imperial swordsman? Why are you looking at me like that?"

Noticing Iska staring from the front seat, Rin twisted her face into a moody scowl.

"Do you suspect this is a fake?"

"That's not it," Iska replied.

"What, then?"

"...I was just thinking that you've gotten friendlier."

"What did you say?!"

She noisily clambered to her feet...

...inside the car. She had leaned forward with such force, she nearly rammed her head right into the skylight.

"You— What do you mean by that?! Are you insinuating that you've won me over?!"

"I meant it as a compliment!" Iska attempted to quickly placate Rin after she angered for some unfathomable reason.

———

The Empire.

East border checkpoint. Easternmost Altoria jurisdiction.

The line of cars and buses waiting for an immigration check stretched on for hundreds of meters.

"What?! There's way too much traffic. What's going on?!" Commander Mismis immediately cried. She leaned out the window and looked at the line of cars. "This is like one of the capital checkpoints. But why would a border crossing at the outskirts of the Empire be so congested...?"

"Could I see?" Rin, who had leaned out the window on the opposite side of the car, was also staring dubiously at the lines of cars. "Are the queues different from during peacetime? Tell me what's going on, Commander Mismis."

"Don't ask me! It just looks oddly busy."

"...You don't think they found out I'm sneaking in?"

"N-no. They couldn't have!"

From the corners of their eyes…

"Hey, Commander, maybe they're doing body checks?" Nene pointed at the cars lined up for the border checkpoint. The immigration officers were calling over passengers into the security inspection area one by one.

"Don't they usually just look over your passport and luggage and make an astral energy check? It seem like they're frisking everyone right now. I think that's what's causing the delays."

"They must've buffed up the inspection requirements," Jhin continued. It seemed he'd grown tired of watching the border crossing and leaned back in his seat. "The Imperial forces made a whole fuss in the Sovereignty and ended up capturing purebreds, so they've got to expect the Sovereignty will send assassins over in retaliation. Of course they're gonna tighten security."

"…I find it quite galling." Rin scowled through her irritation. "Well, it's fine. Bring on the frisking or whatever else they have in store. Although I am disgusted at the thought of Imperial hands touching me, if this is what Lady Sisbell's rescue demands, then so be it."

"So, Rin…"

"What is it, Imperial swordsman?"

"You can act this way around us, but if you get grumpy just because someone's an Imperial at the immigration checkpoint, you're going to arouse suspicion. You need to be mindful of that, at the very least."

"…" Rin was silent.

Was she mad? That was what Iska had thought, at least, but he was immediately disproven.

"Thank you very much for your concern, Mr. Iska." The brown-haired girl gave him an incredibly charming smile.

And her voice was as sweet as a tumbling bell.

"You need not worry about me. I, Rin Vispose, am well aware of how to behave properly, just as I am doing now. I will act the part of a meek traveler."

"............"

"Is there something the matter, Mr. Iska?"

"Well, I was just thinking I'd be ecstatic if you were always this nice."

"Sorry, not happening in a million years."

"You didn't even miss a beat!"

"Yes, it's easily a hundred million times more worthwhile for me to smile at an alley rat over an Imperial," Rin answered with a charming grin.

"Would it kill you to be more polite when you talk with us?!"

Iska sighed at Rin, who'd made no attempts to hide her animosity as she spoke to him.

An hour passed.

"And who was saying not to worry?"

The border checkpoint, in front of the inspection area.

In a parking lot filled with more than a hundred cars, Jhin, who had grown tired of idling, crossed his arms. "We've been waiting thirty minutes since our frisk finished, Iska. I know that it takes a long time for women to dress, but... Hey, Nene. She went in with you for the check, right?"

"That's right. But the commander and I were given priority."

Nene pointed at a security inspection area that had recently been created. Though they were processing men and women separately, Iska and the others had been given priority, since they'd presented their Imperial force IDs.

Rin, who was the only one of their group who would be searched as an ordinary civilian, stood in the gigantic women's line.

"Sure is taking a while."

Commander Mismis was probably unaware she was clutching her left shoulder.

Her astral crest.

Astral energy detectors were in use all over the Empire, so

there was no doubt that the border checkpoint would also have high-performance radar on hand.

"Even if her astral energy isn't seeping out...what happens if the self-adhesive starts coming off during the physical exam and she's caught?"

"If that happens, then that's it. There's no way to protect her. That was the agreement from the start."

Though Jhin's answer sounded cold, he was spot-on. They couldn't be on the Sovereignty's side. In the end, they were just returning home to the Empire, and Rin had simply *tagged along by chance*. If she was caught, their hands would be tied.

Then again...

Worried as Iska was about her, that was the cold hard truth.

"Commander, I'm going to check in on her really quick. Is that okay?"

"In that case, I'll go, too. She should be in the women's line, after all."

Just then, a girl with brown hair exited the security examination area.

"Miss Rin! Oh, I'm so glad..."

"What's wrong, Commander Mismis?"

"Well, you were taking a little while, so we got anxious."

"It was simply crowded," Rin replied. "The examination itself was over in no time flat. It was so easy, it was almost a letdown. Immigration checks are essentially the same no matter where you go."

Evidently, she had undressed during the exam, because she wore only a shirt and pants as she approached. Her jacket hung off her shoulders. She didn't seem to find their concern over her to be necessary.

"What is it, Imperial swordsman? Did you assume I would bungle a simple examination?"

"To be honest, I was a little worried. You were taking a long time, so I thought the astral energy detector might have caught you."

"At this stage? I hid it with a self-adhesive, obviously. There's no chance of astral energy seeping out."

"We were talking about what we would have done if the adhesive peeled off. Since the examination does involve physical contact."

"What? Why would something that would never happen worry you so much?" Rin remained composed as she snorted. "They couldn't discover my astral crest with such a simple physical examination."

"Really?"

"Of course not. They didn't ask me to remove my underwear, so I wasn't afraid they would discover it."

"Oh? That's goo— Wait, your underwear?"

She nodded as though it was only natural. Suddenly, Iska realized something incredibly momentous.

You can't see Rin's astral crest unless she takes off her underwear.

That meant it was on a part of her body that was hidden by her undergarments.

And practically speaking, that meant it had to be...

"Uh?!"

Nene and Commander Mismis, who had made the same realization, both opened their eyes wide.

"It's under your panties?! Which means your astral crest must be... I-is it *there*? ...No, maybe it's *there*!"

"Oh my, oh my! Y-you can't, Commander!" Nene exclaimed. "You're making me feel secondhand embarrassment just mentioning it!"

Commander Mismis started to turn red in the face as her imagination ran wild. Nene was so self-conscious that she covered her ears.

However...

There was one girl who was far more ashamed than either of those two could be.

"............"

Though she still wore a poker face, even Rin's ears were bright red. In an attempt to hold back the humiliation she felt from revealing her embarrassing secret, she stared at her feet and balled her hands into fists.

"Iskaaaaaaaa!" she yelled. She was so mortified that she ran at him while tears were forming in the corners of her eyes. "This time I will not forgive you!"

"For what?!"

"I cannot believe you revealed my secret! You...you asked that question so innocently; that was where you erred. But what's so wrong about having an astral crest on one's buttocks?!"

"People can hear you!"

Rin's astral crest was on her derriere.

You better not say anything.

After Rin made them (read: threatened them to) swear to keep her secret, Iska and the rest of the group passed through the Imperial checkpoint.

3

The Nebulis palace.

The Queen's Palace, surrounded by the Star, Moon, and Solar Spires.

The royal family began filing into the castle's multipurpose hall. Those who sat at the round table were all heads of houses. Alice was attending for the Lou family on behalf of the queen, who had been injured.

Beside them stood their retainers. Combined with the royal guards also occupying the hall, there were likely fifty people in total. It was a gathering of the gentility, of those with the most authority within the superpower, but as the person attending in the queen's stead, Alice viewed the spectacle in an entirely different light.

...These shrewd old foxes are all masters of manipulating conversations.

...Just being here is making it hard to breathe.

The topic of the conference was the restoration of the Sovereignty.

Discussions had already lasted several days. The upper crust needed to explain everything to the citizens, who the Imperial invasion had made uneasy, and most importantly, they needed to deliberate over the rescue of the abducted members of the royal family.

"..."

As her attendant next to her prepared a recording device, Alice glanced over at Rin, or rather, at the girl pretending to be her.

...When she's holding still, she seems the spitting image of Rin.

...As long as she doesn't speak out of turn during the conference, they should be none the wiser.

But just as she had thought that...

"Alice, my dear."

"Y-yes?!"

That address had come from three seats away.

When the head of the Hydra, Talisman, called her name, Alice immediately turned to him.

"Oh, my apologies," he said. "It looks like I've given you a fright."

Clad in a luxurious white suit, he gave her a gentleman's smile. She was impressed he had the gall to speak to her, the daughter of the queen, after leading the assassination plot against her mother himself.

"I see you are wearing new royal garb," he noted.

"...Oh, yes."

"Your previous outfit looked glorious on you, but it seems you've even upstaged that. How splendid. It matches the dignity you hold, Alice."

Had anyone else said that line, she would have responded with a smile for the compliment.

At this moment, Alice was the queen's proxy.

Until then, she had been wearing clothing tailored for a princess. By contrast, the outfit she now wore had been specially fashioned for her new role. Though it had been crafted in the same style as her earlier garb, her new clothes featured more florid red and blue hues.

"I suppose this conference is your debut of the new attire?"

"I'm very grateful for your words. The designer finished putting it together just in time for the conference."

She was lying, of course. Alice had decided to debut her new outfit here, where the other royal family members of the Zoa and Hydra households were gathered, to show them her conviction to act as the queen's proxy.

To show that she would not relinquish her mother's throne.

Of course, Talisman must have realized that himself.

"If I may inquire, Lord Talisman, where is she?" Alice asked.

"You mean Mizy?" One of the princesses was missing. Talisman gave the empty seat a passing glance and smiled wanly. "It happened just a few days ago. Intruders found their way into Snow and Sun and—"

"You mean Salinger, the sorcerer?"

"Yes, indeed. If only we had been able to capture him. He slipped past us, however. I have tasked Mizerhyby with cleaning up after the incident."

"............"

"Well, that's fine enough. It is time. I am sure you are all busy, so let us begin." Talisman, the chairman of the conference, clapped his hands together. He glanced about the round table. "Let us first start with the continuation of yesterday's subject, Defense Minister."

"I shall begin, then." A large, burly man stood up. "The invasion of the Imperial forces. Regarding that incident, we are unsure how they were able to cross the border into the Sovereignty. We believe they passed through the astral trial."

"Just as the documents said."

"Yes, it is believed there are members of the Imperial forces who have transplanted astral crests onto themselves. An Imperial soldier with an astral crest on their arm was witnessed in the battle that took place a few days ago."

An artificial astral crest. None of the people in this room, Alice included, knew whether the Imperial forces had utilized a new type of technology to synthesize one.

...No, one person does.

...Lord Talisman should be aware.

It was vexing. If only Alice could say here and now, *You have ties to the Imperial forces, and you're the one behind everything.* How much relief that would give her.

Until they could retrieve Sisbell, however, she couldn't produce proof that he was the architect of it all.

"Though it is most repugnant to consider," the defense minister continued, "the Imperial forces must indeed have developed astral technology that the Sovereignty has yet to acquire. I may be the defense minister, but I must say that the astral trial isn't sufficient."

"Are you proposing that we replace it with a certificate-of-residence check?" Talisman alone dispassionately nodded along.

"That was what we discussed up to yesterday. If there are no dissenting opinions, we will draw up an official notice today and begin enforcing the resolution at the border checkpoints starting tomorrow at midday."

There were no objections.

"Alice, my dear."

This time, she was called on by Lord Mask from the opposite side of the round table. He gazed at her as she held her tongue.

"As the queen's proxy, or rather, as a princess of the Lou, do you not have an opinion on the matter?"

"…None in particular." She tried her best to remain composed as she coolly agreed with the other cabinet members, refusing to reveal what was actually on her mind. "As for the next item on the agenda—"

"That would be the matter of the Revered Founder."

"Tsk." Alice unintentionally gulped when Lord Mask replied.

"I would like to awaken our Revered Founder."

That had been Lord Mask's proposal during a conference just a few days ago.

He sought vengeance against the Imperial forces—

—from the person who held more authority and astral power than even the queen. If they resuscitated the strongest, oldest astral mage in history, a war would come to fruition—one that could wipe the Empire off the map.

"…It is just as Her Majesty has already said," Alice answered, addressing not only Lord Mask but also the cabinet members closest to the Zoa family and everyone in the room. "We will not entertain the idea of awakening the Revered Founder."

"Hmm. I suppose you are referencing what happened in the neutral city of Ain. I am aware that it sustained some collateral damage when the Revered Founder awakened in the past."

"That is exactly what transpired," Alice replied.

The Founder had returned to her slumber. She was contained within a glass casket that only the queen could open.

"If an astral mage harms any country besides the Empire," Alice asserted, "public opinion would sway in favor of the Empire. We must avoid that at all costs."

Witches and sorcerers.

The world would return to the days of fearing them again if that was to come to pass. They could not allow that to happen.

"I will not give the key to anyone."

"I am well aware. The queen has it, does she not?"

"No, I do."

Suddenly, the atmosphere in the place shifted and tensed in a different way. Their eyes focused on the key in Alice's hand.

"The attempt on the queen's life a few days ago was unsuccessful, but if someone was to attack the queen again and steal the key, we would have a catastrophe on our hands. So it is in my possession."

The key to the Founder's casket. Alice conspicuously put it away in her pocket for all to see.

"Though we have yet to discover the mastermind behind the attempt, I have this to say to them: *If you should like to assault me, by all means, be my guest.*"

If they wanted it, they would need to be prepared for a battle against Aliceliese.

"A wise strategy. Had I been Her Majesty, I daresay I would have done the same." Lord Mask clapped his hands together. "That settles it. We will entrust the matter of the Revered Founder to you, Alice. The Zoa family withdraws our earlier proposal."

"What?"

"Why so surprised?" Lord Mask gave her a thin smile. Behind his metal mask was an inscrutable expression.

"You were against the Revered Founder's awakening yourself," Lord Mask noted.

"...Well, yes," she answered.

She doubted her very own ears. He had backed down on his plan so readily, and it had all been over with so quickly, that Alice almost felt as though she had erred in preparing herself for the matter.

"Are you sure you have nothing else to add, Lord Mask?"

"Why, of course not. I pledge to all those here that I do not."

It was preposterous. Something was clearly amiss. He had submitted too easily. The strange malaise made her feel something bordering on restlessness.

"...I am grateful you have agreed," she said, though ruefully.

CHAPTER 3

Welcome to the Mechanical Utopia

1

United stronghold territory. The Heavenly Empire.

More commonly known as the Empire.

Thanks to their highly mechanized civilization, the country had reached unprecedented levels of glory. People had been calling it a mechanical utopia even a hundred years beforehand.

As a consequence of Founder Nebulis's rebellion, the capital had been razed to ashes.

However...

Yunmelngen, the capital city named after the Lord who ruled the Empire, had been reborn into a steel metropolis. Henceforth, the nation had duly made mechanical advancements in order to prepare for the final war against the witches and sorcerers looming on the horizon.

Or rather...

That was likely the image of the Empire anyone who hadn't ever visited it would have.

"...This is not as described."

A note of irritation and annoyance had entered her voice.

They glided down the highway in a large vehicle as Rin repeated the same line she had already said many times before from the back seat.

"This is not as described. What in the world is this place? Answer me, Imperial swordsman."

"We're definitely in the Empire proper."

"Explain this, then!" Rin pointed out the wide-open window. Instead of a sea of dark-gray buildings, the scenery ahead of the highway consisted of endless green plains, of tranquil pastures. She pointed at cows leisurely grazing in fields bathed in warm sunshine.

"How is this countryside the Empire?!"

"It's obviously the Empire."

"Liar. You are mistaken if you think I know nothing of your nation." Rin didn't stop there. "The Imperial roads are supposed to be mechanized so that all you have to do is get onto a platform to be whisked away to your destination. In place of birds, unmanned aircraft fly through the sky, surveilling the people below. Anyone they find suspicious is immediately shot by automatons with sniper rifles…"

"Not a single one of those things is true!"

"Then what is this place?! Where are the buildings that tower over the Empire like mountains?!"

"They're—," Iska started.

"That's because we're in the outskirts…I think."

That had come from the back seat. Commander Mismis, sitting next to Rin, offered timidly, "There are a lot of large cities like what you're describing, Miss Rin, but I suppose you could say the area where we are now hasn't changed. It probably has the same atmosphere as it did before the Empire assimilated surrounding nations into itself."

Pasture stretched on for as far as the eye could see. In the hour they'd been in the car, they glimpsed roads here and there, but there hadn't been a skyscraper in sight.

Imperial territory. Easternmost Altoria jurisdiction.

They were near the eastern tip of the Empire.

"Come to think of it, Jhin, Nene, and I are from the Imperial capital, but you're from the east, aren't you, Commander Mismis?"

"That's right. But I didn't live this far out in the country."

"Mm-hmm." Meanwhile, Rin turned from absentmindedly watching the cattle at pasture to staring straight below Commander Mismis's neck. "...So that's how they got as big as a cow's."

"Miss Rin! Where do you think you're looking as you say that?!" Upon noticing Rin's gaze, she hid her chest with her hands.

"That makes sense!"

"Now you, Nene?!" Mismis exclaimed.

"You're making the wrong comparison. It's her head you should be considering. She's more carefree and happy-go-lucky than any cow."

"Now you, Jhin?! ...You're terrible, Iska! So you only brought up where I'm from so everyone could make fun of me?!"

"Why the heck would I do that?!"

It was a ridiculous accusation, and groundless at that.

He needed to prove his innocence. Just as he was trying to figure out a way to do it, someone interrupted him.

"All right. That's enough joking around." Rin, who had been staring out the window, sighed loudly as she fell back in her seat. "In other words, I'm not headed to a large city like the Imperial capital. Is that right, Commander Mismis?"

"N-no. Though there are large cities in between, of course."

"Why not?" Rin asked. Her question wasn't directed at anyone from Unit 907. Given that she was looking at the sun earring she held, she was likely asking herself that.

"We can only trust in this signal...but why would they not take Lady Sisbell to a city?"

Indeed.

Iska and the others were headed a great distance from the

Imperial capital toward the eastern outskirts, which was a far cry from the Empire's reputation as a mechanical utopia.

"If they were taking Lady Sisbell as a prisoner of war, they would have moved her to the Imperial headquarters. And the headquarters are in the city. Is that correct?"

"It's exactly where they say it is. I don't know any more than you do," Iska didn't hesitate to reply to Rin as she gazed at him. "The Imperial assembly and the headquarters are both in the Imperial capital. Even the main office of the Empire's sole institute for astral power research, Omen, is there, too."

All the authority was concentrated in one place. That was how the Empire had been organized. Iska had to be careful not to give her additional information, but this was publicly known worldwide.

...But Rin is right to be dubious.

...Sisbell is a purebred. The headquarters and Imperial assembly were both desperate to have one.

Iska assumed she would have been taken to the Imperial capital as well.

But the signal had been in the far eastern part of the Empire, coming from the farthest reaches of its territory—here.

"Hey, Jhin Big Bro, what do you think?"

When Nene addressed him from the driver's seat, the sniper lifted his head. "Hmm? You want to trade places?" he asked.

"That's not it. I want to know why you think they took Miss Sisbell into the countryside rather than to the capital."

"That's not part of our agreement." Jhin shook his head.

He kept his head propped up on his hand as he leaned on the window.

"We're just heading back to the capital. On the way, we'll just *happen* to make a detour to where Sisbell is being held. After that, it's none of our business, and we're not interfering with anything else. And we're not going out of our way to investigate anything, either."

"...Well, yeah, I know that, but..." Nene was hemming and hawing. This wasn't like her.

"We're Imperial soldiers," she said. "Aren't you curious? As a member of the Imperial army? I mean, Miss Sisbell is supposed to be a purebred—she's super rare. If they took her anywhere but the capital, there's no way they'd be able to really get the most out of her."

"No, I'm sure they took her here because they *want* to make full use of her."

"What?"

"..." Jhin glanced to his left.

His eyes met Rin's as her gaze bored into him. He let out a large sigh.

"...Oh, c'mon. Now, this is just my personal opinion, all right?" he prefaced. "So there was that fishy guy. The head of the Hydra or whatever."

Jhin looked up at the roof of the car. It was as though he was recalling the face of the man who had claimed to be Talisman, leader of the Hydra, during the attack on the Lou's villa.

"He's got connections with the Empire without a doubt. But even if he's got them, that doesn't mean he's the real person we're up against."

"...What do you mean by that?"

"He must have handed Sisbell off to somebody in the Empire. Wouldn't it be plausible for his partner to not be part of the head-quarters or the Imperial assembly? In that case, they'd obviously take her far away from the Imperial capital to a place like this."

"............" Rin was silent.

Jhin ignored her as he directed his gaze back out the window.

"Just so you know, I've got no clue who he could have made this deal with. But you can figure out what they're after, yeah? Nene was basically right. Sisbell is a valuable purebred. And since she is, somebody wants to monopolize her—without HQ or the Imperial assembly being any wiser."

"...And you're saying that we're headed to those people?"

"More than likely," Jhin mused. "I'll say it again: This is none of our business. We'll drop you off at wherever they took Sisbell and then head back to the capital. We're not digging into this."

"Fine by me," Rin answered very seriously.

When she said that, this time Jhin was the one taking a look at her.

"Aren't you going to say it's more convenient that way?"

"...What is?"

"The Imperial capital would be hell for you, seeing as how you're from the Sovereignty and all. We've got astral energy detectors set up all over the place and way more military police to boot. Plus, there are so many Saint Disciples there that you'd practically bump shoulders with them."

"What? How idiotic. You think I'm relieved that we are not headed to the capital?" Rin dramatically crossed her arms. "It's actually a letdown. I have been prepared to set foot there ever since I was ordered to rescue Lady Sisbell. But now that the time has come, we're headed to the countryside instead."

"You sound awfully confident."

"I'm not exaggerating. I bet you haven't even begun to realize the experience I have."

I'm tired of being in the car. As though she were trying to imply that simply through her firm tone of voice, Rin addressed the driver. "Nene, or whoever you are, will we reach the location today?"

"Maybe by tomorrow," she replied. "We're almost at a large town, so we'll stay there overnight. We also need to charge the car soon."

"...Well, no matter," Rin said offhandedly, almost brazenly.

"I thought I was in for some shocking sights, but that was when I believed we were headed for the capital instead of the Imperial boonies."

2

Imperial territory. Easternmost Altoria jurisdiction.

Nata City.

Travelers taking the highway used this town as a stopover for the night. Much like Ain, it was filled with many charming historic structures. Here, tourists could leisurely pass the time away from the hustle and bustle of the city.

At the moment, however, there was one person who was the polar opposite of relaxed.

"Miss Rin! You're too close to my back, and even if I was okay with you latching onto my shoulders like that, you're gripping so tight it hurts!"

"...I—I can't help it!"

It was a weekday evening. Unit 907 stood out among the large crowd. Or rather, Rin stood out.

"I need to do this so I can keep watch. Please cooperate with me, Commander Mismis!"

Despite being taller than Mismis, Rin had latched onto the woman's back and was restlessly observing her surroundings. She would take a step, then stop, then take another before halting again. On top of that, since she was openly glaring at the businesspeople and tourists passing by, everyone else was putting more and more distance between themselves and Iska's group.

"So all the people walking down this road are Imperial subjects, I presume?" Rin said. "I cannot allow any of them to know my identity!"

"They're going to think you're suspicious *because* you're acting jumpy!"

"Hng?! They're...moving away from me? What is the meaning of this, Commander?"

"It's because *you're* staring, Miss Rin!"

For once, Commander Mismis was doing the teasing. This was absolutely priceless for Iska and the rest of the unit.

"Hey, Iska, Nene." Jhin, who was at the edge of the road, motioned for them to move closer. "You guys come over here. If we're near those two, we'll start looking suspicious, too."

"Really, Jhin?!" Mismis complained.

"...Oh, c'mon. And you were saying that being in the country-side was a letdown?" He sighed. "If you're quivering in your boots out in the sticks, you wouldn't be able to even walk down a road in the capital. You'd look so suspicious that the military police would ask to check your ID right then and there, and it would all be over."

"Jhin Big Bro, she's kind of like one of those puppies that'll howl themselves hoarse in a cage but cower as soon as you let them out..."

"Wh-what did you say?!" Rin quickly scowled when she caught Jhin and Nene whispering to each other. "Did you compare me to a frightened little whelp? Nonsense!"

"Please don't shout while you're right behind me!"

"Guh...h-hey, *you* there!" Rin was looking at Iska. She had promised earlier not to call him *Imperial swordsman* in town. "I-Isk......"

But for whatever reason, Rin had trouble saying his name even when she was staring directly at him. Even making good eye contact with him was proving difficult, and her face was turning a deeper and deeper shade of red, almost as though she was holding her breath.

"...I feel an odd resistance to addressing you by your name in public," she said.

"Huh? Why's that?"

"You, with the black hair!"

"That's even worse!" Iska moaned.

"Sh-shut up. I simply find it vexing to utter your name..." Rin breathed out. "How deep into this place are you planning on taking me? We have almost walked the entirety of the main street."

"We're headed to Restaurant Row up ahead. According to this pamphlet, they recommend—"

"What?! ...Do you intend to disgrace me by taking me to somewhere no one finds popular?! You freak!"

"Could you listen to me?!" Iska shouted.

This was futile. Iska's shoulders drooped as he realized Rin's first excursion to the Empire was making her too anxious to listen.

They headed to the café terrace of Albireo, a chain that boasted many locations throughout the Empire. There were several in the Imperial capital, so Iska would often go there for a quick bite to eat.

"It's an interesting restaurant. They call themselves a café even though their tea and coffee aren't great, but their stews and curries are good enough to make up for that. I go there for lunch a lot, too, and—"

They were inside the establishment, which was bustling during the dinnertime rush.

At the six-seat table, Commander Mismis opened the menu with familiar ease. She propped up the menu so Rin could see it from across from her.

"This egg sandwich is really fluffy, and they use top-grade shrimp stock to give the au gratin some extra oomph. And don't even get me started about the pancakes! Oh, and I can't forget to mention that they're staunch about only cooking once an order has been put in."

"..."

"Restaurant Row has some of the Empire's older eateries, but we thought it'd be easier for you to have dinner here, Miss Rin. I also recommend the cream soda. They heap the whipped cream on top and... Miss Rin?"

A river of sweat broke out on Rin's forehead before Mismis's eyes.

"...Whew...whew...get it together," she muttered to herself.

Just like when she'd been out in the main street, it seemed Rin didn't have the capacity to wipe her sweat away while in this restaurant, either. She was preoccupied with observing the movements of the other guests around her and the waitstaff rather than the menu.

"Nene, or whoever you are, you were saying that you're good with machines, correct?" Rin asked.

"Hmm? Well, I guess you could say that."

"What is that surveillance camera over there?" she surreptitiously whispered into Nene's ear, gazing at the camera on the ceiling. "Does the Empire even have surveillance in restaurants like this?"

"That's just a normal security camera. I think it's there to discourage people from robbing them."

"...But what if...?" Rin almost got right under the device and stared up at it. "Are you sure it's not there specifically to keep an eye on me? What if the Empire has caught wind of my incursion, and they are employing the pursuit systems they had installed already...?"

"You're overthinking things! You'll be fine, so please calm down!"

"B-but," Rin started to object. She faltered as Nene began shaking her shoulders. "I would personally feel much safer if we could destroy the thing..."

"You'd be arrested for destruction of private property!"

"I—I would?"

"You don't have to be so scared about being out in the open, Miss Rin. We'll hold up our promise," Nene assured her. "None of us would betray you, okay? Here, take the entrée menu."

"......I see."

She stared intently at Nene, who was offering her one of the menus. Rin nodded weakly.

"That's true. In some ways, I've become overly sensitive because

I am carrying the weight of such a hefty mission. I must act more natural."

"That's right! Act more like a tourist!"

"Mm-hmm." Rin seemed to have finally gotten over her nerves.

Or rather, right before she was able to relax, she heard the clack of an unfamiliar footfall come from behind her.

"Are you ready to order—?"

"I feel someone behind me!" Rin leaped out of her seat. "Has the enemy finally arrived?!"

Iska didn't even have the time to stop her as she unleashed an explosive roundhouse kick behind her.

Thunk.

Rin's heel made a pleasing sound as it connected directly with the waiter's head.

"Oh......"

The man she had kicked wore a name tag that read, EMPLOYEE SUPERVISOR.

"Oh, oh no! I moved on reflex!"

"What do you think you're doing?!"

Iska quickly caught the employee, who had collapsed, half unconscious.

"Nene, fix this quick."

"Uh-uh-huh! But other people around us saw..."

"...No, it's fine. The kick was so fast, they couldn't have caught it. We can cover this up!" Iska asserted just as another waitress came over from the back in what had to have been the worst timing ever.

"Oh, Manager, you're playing hooky and sitting in a customer's seat? That's sooo unfair."

"No, no, nothing's happening! I—I know him, and we haven't spoken in a while, so I wanted to sit and catch up... Uh, ah-ha-ha..." Commander Mismis distracted the waitress.

Jhin followed up by slamming down all the water on the table.

"Anyway, we're out of water. Could we get a refill?"

"Oh, yes. I'll have it right away. Manager, if you keep sitting out of work for things like this, I'll tattle on you to the execs."

She grinned and left.

Just as Iska had anticipated, for better or worse, there apparently hadn't been any witnesses.

"Phew. Somehow, we've managed to—"

"Don't let your guard down, Iska." Just as he was wiping away the cold sweat he had broken out in, Rin, the perpetrator herself, reminded him. "As long as I'm in the Empire, unforeseen events like what happened just now will continue to transpire over and over again. In fact, I'm positive I will stir up an incident to surpass this one."

"Why are you positive about something so negative?!"

"Steel yourself for it!"

"Why're you making it sound suave?!"

Iska looked from the defiant Rin to the unconscious manager, then stared back at the other members of his unit behind him.

3

They had finished dinner.

Late night, twelfth floor of the hotel.

The hallway was dead silent. In the meeting area at the end of the hall, Iska sipped a canned coffee.

"…We really made it back to the Empire."

He glanced ahead at the vending machine from which he had purchased the beverage.

The coin slot took Imperial currency. He couldn't use the shared paper currency of the rest of the world. That was probably because the machine was Imperial-made, meant for use only within the Empire. The newspapers it stocked were also published by Imperial companies. Their articles all featured headlines about the Empire, which filled him with nostalgia.

If there was one thing that seemed out of place, though...

"...This is definitely nothing like the capital."

The scenery the hotel looked out upon was a far cry from the familiar sights of the Imperial capital. Here on the remote eastern edge of the Empire, the near-futuristic buildings of that city were nowhere to be found.

Three AM.

The town was deserted, its residents asleep. Even the hallways of the hotel were empty, save for Iska, who was on guard outside the room.

"............"

He took another swig from the coffee can.

Of course, if Jhin had been around, he would have pointed out that Iska was behaving unusually. He typically refrained from taking stimulants voluntarily unless he was eating in the company of others.

In other words, he was so mentally and physically exhausted that he had needed a small amount of caffeine.

...But I was just lying down. And I just traded places keeping watch with Jhin.

...I can't believe I'm still sleepy.

He knew the reason why.

Now that he was back home, he had subconsciously let his guard down. There was the fatigue he had endured from being in the Nebulis Sovereignty, an enemy nation, and being home had likely dispelled all tension he once had felt.

"Come to think of it, even Jhin fell asleep right away without reading for once. I guess everyone else is feeling this, too."

Their long journey would soon end, and they now had a clear goal. They would take Rin to her destination. Once that was done, they would cleanly cut ties with the Sovereignty.

"I was worried how this would go at the start, but Rin's been behaving."

Things had been uneventful post-dinner. All the ruckus she'd made during the daytime had probably tuckered her out. Rin had grown quiet after arriving at the hotel. She was probably sound asleep at this very moment.

Or so Iska thought.

Ka-chak. The door to her room gingerly opened right in front of him.

"Iska..."

"Rin? I thought you were asleep... Whoa, why are your eyes red?!"

Rin unsteadily poked her head from out the door.

Though he had been convinced she was sleeping, she was still wearing the same suit as earlier. What's more, she looked pale with fatigue, and her eyes were bloodshot, as though she'd been awake all night.

"Wait, you weren't asleep?"

"..........." Rin nodded firmly in affirmation. "I shouldn't have gotten my own room. As soon as I was on my own in this Imperial hotel, it felt more and more like I was being watched..."

"You're being way too cautious!"

"This is the Empire we're in. There could be bugs and hidden cameras all over my accommodations..."

"You don't have to worry about that," Iska assured her.

"...That's just it." The tired brown-haired girl motioned for him to approach. "Despite the shame I feel, I will tell you this. There's something I'd like you to help me with..."

"You want me to just sweep the room? Like to make sure there aren't any suspicious devices in it?"

"Your guess is spot-on."

"Well, we've had similar experiences. I did that at the estate."

He was referring to the Lou family's villa. The experience of checking for anything that seemed like a camera in his unit's lodgings was still fresh in his mind.

...Back then, Sisbell also said there weren't any.

...So I can understand how Rin feels.

"I got it. I can help with that, at least."

He headed into her quarters. Beginning the sweep with the living room, he found that it was surprisingly clean. Then again, that was probably because she had been too hesitant to use anything.

"I don't see any suspicious mechanisms behind the curtains or near the outlets. No small holes in the walls, either. See, it's like I told you. Just your run-of-the-mill hotel room."

"...Okay, I get it. I'll agree that there isn't anything set up in here." Rin relaxed. "I can finally use it."

"Well, that's what's important. I'll go back to guard duty, then..."

"There's something else, too."

"Huh?"

"We're leaving at six AM, right? That's barely three hours away."

He'd already finished the inspection for her.

Rin pulled out her towel from her suitcase right in front of Iska as he watched, puzzled. It was large enough to wrap around her whole body.

"I am Lady Alice's attendant. To serve the royal family, I must always keep my hygiene in order. That means I need to maintain my personal appearance."

"And what exactly are you asking for from me?"

"...For this." Rin pointed at the bathroom. It was probably just his imagination, but she looked both pale and flushed at the same time. "I have some business to attend to in there. You understand, I take it?"

"......Yes. So you're saying I should make myself scarce, right?"

"Tsk!" Rin shot a glare at him.

He thought he had been considerate, but it seemed that hadn't been what she had been aiming for. She squeezed the towel in her hands.

"So, um…come on! How do you not get it?!"

"Get what?"

"Guuuh! Seriously! I want you to keep watch over my accommodations while I'm in the bath. That's what I mean!" Rin howled. "Obviously, I'm defenseless in there. Even if this place isn't tapped, the Imperial forces could very well rush in on an innocent girl like me."

"No way that'd happen!"

"I'm asking for this just in case. Until I finish bathing, I'd like you to watch over the room and my personal effects."

"…Okay, I'll bite. Are you serious?"

"Of course. I don't plan on telling anyone else about this, either. We can keep this between you and me." Still clutching the towel, Rin turned her back to him. Or so he thought, until she half turned around like she had remembered something. "You wait here. If you so much as touch the bathroom door, I'll treat you like the animal you are for the rest of your life."

"I'd never."

"You're not allowed to sniff the steam coming from here, either."

"Do you take me for a pervert?!"

"Anyway, just wait here like I've told you… I will specially allow you to partake of some of the fine tea I've brought with me. Please pour yourself a cup."

Rin quickly headed into the bathroom. After she left, he found the tea set on the table.

"…Maybe she noticed I was drinking coffee."

This was essentially his reward for keeping watch. She was being considerate in her own way by offering him something superior to the crude coffee he had been sipping.

"Still, having tea right after canned coffee… Though I guess she'd be mad at me if I didn't have any. *I see. So the tea I brought was unappetizing*, she'd say while glaring at me…"

He'd down a cup just to avoid having her grousing at him.

Iska opened the bag of tea and filled the kettle that came with the room with water, then waited.

Thunk.

Just then, he heard something heavy fall.

"...What was that just now?"

It was a dull noise. This could have just been his imagination, but it sounded a lot like it had come from the bathroom, where Rin had headed into.

"Rin? I heard a crash."

He received no reply. Perhaps that was because the door was closed or because she couldn't hear him over the noise of the running shower.

...That wasn't a gentle noise, either.

...It sounded heavy, like dozens of pounds heavy.

She had asked him to keep watch. In light of that, he couldn't just ignore what he'd heard.

"Rin? Hey, Rin!"

Getting as close to the bathroom door as he could, Iska called her name. He received no answer.

He could hear the shower beyond the entrance, but she still hadn't responded at all.

"Hey, Rin?! ...Can you really not hear me?! Listen, in five seconds, I'm going to open this door if I don't get a response!"

The five seconds went by in the blink of an eye. Gulping, he placed his hand on the doorknob.

The bathroom.

Beyond the glass wall that was clouded with heat and vapor, he could vaguely make out a girl still holding the shower nozzle, slumped against the wall.

"Rin?! ...Are you okay?!" he knocked on the glass and yelled, but she remained slouched over, facedown.

Was she unconscious?

"That's enough! You better not get mad at me later!"

He grabbed one of the prearranged bath towels and opened the glass door.

"Rin!"

Amid the bright white steam, she sat unmoving on the floor. He wrapped her naked form in the bath towel and picked her up.

"…Uh…" The sopping-wet girl let a sigh slip out.

She'd likely gotten dizzy from a combination of her fatigue and the heat.

…Is it because she's been nervous ever since coming to the Empire? But it's barely been a day.

…In that case, she's probably been exhausted since way before.

When he thought back on it, Rin had regularly been burdened with responsibilities ever since they were in the Sovereignty. She had performed as both Alice's attendant and guard. She had participated in the plan to infiltrate Snow and Sun and arranged things so it would play out perfectly. Unit 907 hadn't been the only ones who'd been feeling stretched thin.

"Rin, I'm going to take you to the living room."

Iska carried the towel-clad girl and laid her on the sofa.

He would need to watch over her after that. If he didn't see any improvement, would he go to the hotel infirmary? No, considering she was unclothed, there was a small but real chance they would realize she was a witch.

"It'd be best if Commander Mismis or Nene woke her up. She'd probably think it was weird if she saw me…"

"Uh, ugh…"

The brown-haired girl weakly opened her eyes.

"Rin?! Oh, good. I had no idea what to do."

"…………"

Rin sat up from her horizontal position.

She stared for a while at herself and the bath towel wrapped around her. Then she rubbed the back of her head, which she seemed to have bumped.

"I was..."

Rin got up from the sofa. Ensuring she had a secure hold on the bath towel that just barely covered her, she quickly pushed aside her wet bangs.

"......I see." She nodded meekly. "That was a blunder on my part. I cannot believe I lost consciousness while bathing."

"I'm glad I realized you had. Do you know why it happened? I think you were so tired that—"

"Please, do not say it. I have gathered what occurred." Rin interrupted Iska, then continued. "This is how things played out: You're so depraved that once you knew I was bathing, you took the opportunity to assault me suddenly from behind."

"......Come again?"

"And then you took me to the sofa in order to take advantage of me."

"W-wait, hold on! I think there's been a huge misunderstanding—"

"There has been no such thing!"

The dripping-wet girl took a large step forward. Though the force of her movement exposed her strong thighs, she was so incensed that she didn't notice.

"Are you trying to claim that I collapsed in the bath of all places, and from dizziness at that? ...There is no way I could have let something so embarrassing happen to me!"

"You know exactly what happened, then!"

"...Guh. I cannot believe this."

Drip. A water droplet fell from the tip of her hair as Rin gritted her teeth.

"For an Imperial of all people to glimpse my shame...when only my father has seen me like this...and then for that same Imperial to move me from there to here..."

"L-like I said, I had to!"

"I am well aware. I don't blame you." Rin gritted her teeth

again. She pressed her hand against her breast, which was hidden by the towel. "However, Iska, I must tell you something important."

"Wh-what...?"

"You cannot think that what you saw was all that I am. Though even Lady Sisbell has overtaken me, I will surely outgrow her someday!"

"What?!"

"I will not always be as flat as a great plain. Someday, I shall reach the same level as Lady Alice, and then I will eventually be as marvelous as Lady Elletear!"

"...Can I leave now?"

"Oh, don't you dare run away from this! Listen, if you speak of my bosom, I will never forgive y—"

Still wearing the bath towel, Rin pursued Iska. He sprinted away from the girl, who was ranting at him with a vigor that far outdid any previous rants of hers.

Several hours later.

The morning of their second day in the Empire.

"Wait, Iska. There's something we still need to do in town."

"Hmm?"

"Please come this way."

They were right outside the hotel. As Iska had been headed to the parking lot, Rin pulled him aside by motioning at him.

"You need something?" he asked.

"Over here. Come with me."

Rin was headed to the commercial street. It was the opposite direction of the hotel parking lot.

"Everyone's already waiting in the parking lot," he told her. "Shouldn't we hurry up and get to Sisbell?"

"It'll take a few minutes at most."

Rin strode gallantly down the main road. She had settled slightly compared to the day before, when she'd been hiding in Commander Mismis's shadow. As she walked alongside Iska, it almost seemed like there was a spring in her step.

"Actually, Rin, I know I'm only asking now, but did you change back into your old clothes?"

"Suits are too stiff. I am much more used to this outfit."

She had gone back to wearing her housekeeping uniform. However, it was slightly different from the clothes Iska had seen her in up to now. In a nutshell, it looked like they had been designed for mobility.

"I decided on this outfit after getting a sense of the Empire for myself. Of its fashion, I mean."

"What do you mean by that?"

"If I am dressed as a housekeeper, no one will think me suspicious. I probably look like nothing more than a waitress from a café walking down the street."

Indeed.

She must have come to that realization from her experience eating dinner the night before.

...But she was practically cowering from the stress then.

...I guess she was keeping an eye on the things that counted in the Imperial streets.

He supposed he should have expected that from her, seeing as she would never allow herself to make any oversights. Then again, as one of the Imperials being observed, he had mixed feelings about the whole thing.

"I am not the only one with new garb. Lady Alice has also made a wardrobe change."

"She has?" When Rin mentioned that in passing, Iska stopped in his tracks unintentionally and repeated her statement. "Alice's clothes? You mean she's wearing something different from her royal dress?"

"...Oh no." Rin put her hand over her mouth. She'd accidentally let something slip. Now that Iska knew, however, he couldn't just leave it at that.

"I must stress that this cannot reach anyone else," Rin said. "Not even your three colleagues."

"I wouldn't tell them. I won't, but..."

Now he was curious. The white royal garb that Aliceliese Lou Nebulis IX wore was custom-made for her. But now she wasn't wearing it anymore? What caused her to need to do that?

"Interested? I won't tell you, though. This solely concerns Lady Alice and the royal family. I cannot reveal anything to an Imperial soldier."

"I get that. I'm not going to launch an investigation into it or anything."

Rin could have lied to him anyway. The fact that she had straightforwardly told him she couldn't discuss it with an Imperial soldier was the greatest confession she could make. For now, all he could do was speculate.

...If this were the Imperial forces, changing her uniform so abruptly would mean a huge promotion.

...But is that what happened to Alice? What's above a princess?

The only title that came to mind was queen, but there was no way. Or maybe there was another reason for the change of outfit?

"Hmm."

"Ha-ha, I take it you're racking your brain to figure it out?" Rin asked.

"...Well, I can't think of a reason why she'd change clothes. Anyway, I'd like to ask you about something else instead. Where are we headed?"

They were already in the thick of the shopping district. They had left the hotel far behind. If they kept walking, they would also be well past the parking lot where Jhin, Nene, and Commander Mismis were waiting.

"This will do." Rin stopped in the middle of the main thoroughfare. There were, of course, many pedestrians. Right in the center of everything, she pulled out a high-grade digital camera from her bag.

"Yes," she said. "I'll start with that conspicuous building."

Then she snapped a picture. She took photo upon photo of the bustling streets immediately outside the hotel.

"Mementos of my time here," she told Iska. "Since I am a tourist, after all."

"...Right. I suppose you are."

It sounded exactly like what a spy would say if, for instance, the military police took them aside. If she was going to pretend to be a tourist, then naturally she would need to have taken a photo or two of the Empire.

"...Personally, I'm a little uneasy about you going about your spy activities in front of me," Iska commented.

"This isn't classified information, so I don't see how you could take issue with it. The photos I am shooting hardly differ from those in public Imperial travel guides."

"Well, I guess they don't..."

"Hmph. You sure have a lot to complain about. Fine, I'll snap a different type of picture, then."

Rin sighed.

Or so he thought. Instead, she put her hand on his shoulder and pulled him close to her. She turned the camera lens at them, and...

"Uhhh?!"

"Don't struggle or it'll be out of focus."

She took a selfie of the two of them together. A photo of a young man and woman in the main street of a tourist town. Iska came out slightly blurry, since he'd been moving.

"...Now, this may sound odd for me to say, but people are going to get the wrong idea from this picture," he told her.

"It's an important shot," Rin insisted in an entirely serious tone as she immediately checked the selfie they had just taken. "This shows that I have entered the Empire safely and that you are accompanying me as promised. This picture will let me kill two birds with one stone."

"Wait, are you sending it to Alice?!"

"Obviously." Rin shrugged at him. "I am certain I am causing her a great deal of worry right now. She's forced her most beloved attendant to fight her way through enemy territory alone, after all."

"...Alone? I think we've been helping you out a whole lot, too."

"When we passed through the Imperial checkpoint," Rin continued, "those three military vehicles pursuing us from behind put up a dangerous fight."

"How much are you planning on embellishing?!"

"I'll keep it reasonable."

Rin rapidly operated the digital camera, pressing a complicated sequence of buttons that weren't on any of the models up for sale.

"There. I've finished sending it. Now, don't worry yourself over this. I sent her our selfie together. There isn't a shred of secret information from the Empire in it."

"A picture of my face? I feel kind of weird having Alice see that..."

"What? What are you talking about? What is important is *my* face."

She put her camera into her bag. Once she had fulfilled her objective, she looked up at the sky in satisfaction.

"I am certain that Lady Alice will be pleased to know I am safe."

───────────

The Nebulis palace. Star Spire.

The princess's private chambers.

"...You look oddly pleased," Alice murmured, head propped up in her hands and wearing an incredibly strange expression. She held a small monitor. Displayed on it was the scene of a town she did not recognize. This was one of the pictures Rin had taken of the Imperial streets. Alice didn't mind that aspect of the photo. She was, of course, happy to see Rin safe and sound, and she had certainly gained some pluck after learning details of their pursuit of Sisbell.

"...Ngh." No, it was the selfie of Rin and Iska that Alice was glaring at. "Rin, aren't you a little *too* close to Iska?"

There were more pictures. Scenes of them both walking together. Photos of him eating at a café that she'd snuck from close proximity.

She'd probably been acting out to avoid the others catching on to her.

Alice got that. She understood full well that this was necessary on her attendant's part.

"Ugh! I'm always telling you, though, Rin. Iska is supposed to be mine..."

She had started fidgeting. She simply couldn't help but be concerned about what Iska was doing with the opposite sex without her, his rival.

...Well, it is Rin, after all.

...It is what it is. I trust that this won't turn into a Sisbell situation.

She had felt something similar in the past.

Back when Iska had held her little sister's hand.

At the time, her sister had actually come to steal him from her. Alice had started to feel rather murderous then, so this was tolerable by comparison.

"But you know what, Rin? You can't get any closer to Iska. I cannot permit it."

Alice shook her head at the small monitor.

Rin hadn't heard that, of course.

"Even if that isn't what you intend. You are in a distant land, in the Empire, together, alone. If you do that..."

A scene flashed into Alice's mind.

As if I could leave you alone. I'll always be by your side.

Imperial swordsman…no, Iska. Are you sure? Are you certain you want a woman like me…?

Rin, quivering with anxiety over being in the Empire. And Iska, supporting her. Though she would refuse his kindness at first, eventually Rin would open her heart to him, and the distance between them would diminish.

"But then…forbidden feelings could bud between them, over-coming even the fact that they are enemies. No, I'm certain those sensations have sprouted already!"

The two of them would eventually come to a decision.

They would elope.

Bye, Alice; good-bye, Lady Alice—that was all they would say to her before heading off to a land far from the Sovereignty and the Empire to dwell in a den of love for only the two of them.

"How utterly sordid!"

Alice flung away the monitor as she tore at her hair.

"Romance between a person of the Sovereignty and one from the Empire. Preposterous! I cannot abide it!"

Perhaps…the two of them had made *progress* out of the camera frame? That is, they had passed into the adult world.

"M-maybe…they have even kissed… Oh, ahhh! No, no, no! I cannot simply stand by and let this happen. I must tell Rin that she is forbidden from engaging in further shamelessness—"

"What is forbidden?"

"Yeek?!"

Alice jumped involuntarily at someone speaking to her from behind. When she cautiously turned around, she found the queen in a nightgown.

"Alice, I cannot condone you making such a commotion at night. What shall we do if the guards in the hall were to overhear?"

"I-I'm so sorry, Mother!"

She quickly hid the monitor behind her back.

...That was close. She doesn't know about Iska.

...If she was to ask who the boy in the photo is, I would be in such a predicament.

The queen was combing through her hair with her fingers to dry it out. She had just been in the bathroom past the living room ten minutes earlier. It seemed she had already returned from the bath.

Considering how quick the queen had been, Alice doubted she'd spent enough time there.

"Mother, are you done already?"

"Old habits die hard. The bathroom is cramped and enclosed, visibility is low from the steam, and I was unarmed. I would have been in quite the pickle had I been attacked."

"You have me, Mother."

"Of course." The queen, who was flushed from the bath, smiled slightly. "Though as your mother, I would rather not force you to shoulder this burden. I have been inviting myself into your chambers every night, after all."

"It's fine. I feel at ease knowing you are with me at night."

Let's sleep together for the next few days. Alice had proposed that as a defensive measure the night before.

...Mother is still injured.

...And I do not have Rin, either. It's much better to be together at night.

Their astral powers had high compatibility as well. Though Alice's Ice was resilient in the face of bullets and explosions, the walls she created could not ward off airborne contaminants such as tear gas or smoke. The queen's Wind astral power, on the other hand, could easily sweep away such things.

"Mother, would you like something to drink?"

"No, I am fine. We must wake early tomorrow, so I will borrow the bed now, if I may."

"Please do. I will drink a glass of milk and then come right to sleep."

The queen headed to bed.

Alice watched her mother's fluttering golden hair, which was so similar to her own, then sighed in relief. It seemed she hadn't noticed the monitor Alice had hidden behind her back.

"...Phew. That was close."

She opened her living room closet and stashed the monitor away. That had been her preferred hiding spot for years. Only Alice and Rin knew of it. Incidentally, she had an entirely different place where she hid things she wanted to keep secret even from Rin.

A place that her attendant would not stay for long even if she happened to set foot in it. And that place was...

"Oh, what have we here?" The queen's voice came from Alice's bedroom. "Alice, what is this?"

"What's wrong, Mother?"

"Nothing at all. I simply righted the pillow, since it was askew, and found this below it."

The queen was standing beside the bed holding a portable screen. It was different from the one Alice had hidden in the living room.

"...Oh—"

Oh no.

Before she could say those words, Alice scrambled to stop herself.

This was bad. That monitor contained forbidden footage. Though no one was supposed to know about it, the queen was the last person she would have wanted to lay eyes on it.

"M-Mother, that's—!"

"Hmm...I believe I have seen this before." Her mother tilted the screen quizzically. "Oh, it's the computer that saves the footage from the safe house's security camera. So you had it, Alice."

"N-no...um...it...it's a little......"

"?"

"Mother!" Alice shouted, her mind made up. "I—I wanted to use it! Um, so please give—"

She was too late. Before Alice could reach out, the queen had already pressed the button to play the footage. A boy and a girl appeared on-screen. One of them was Rin. The other was Iska, but the queen would have been unfamiliar with him. The issue with the footage Alice had recently been watching every evening was...

"Um...I was taking a shower..."

"Wh-wh-what do you think you're doing?! I-I'm...seventeen years old! A young maiden! And you're an exhibitionist!"

The footage had been taken about a week ago at the Lou's safe house.

As the queen watched the monitor, the scene of the buck-naked black-haired boy was undoubtedly burning itself into her retinas.

His body was slender yet toned. His hair was wet. The droplets coming from the ends of his hair rolled down the muscles of his neck and glistened, giving him a dubious sense of maturity.

"Th-this is?!" the queen exclaimed in surprise. Perhaps from the suddenness of it all, she was unable to peel her eyes away from the shocking footage. "Alice, were you keeping such a vivid image of a man in the nude under your pillow...? What is the meaning of this?!"

The queen's face was slightly red.

I cannot believe my daughter would do this.

How could she secretly take footage of a naked man?

This was the first time Alice's mother had stared at her like this. It was shocking.

"I-it isn't like that! Wait, Mother... Um, yes, that's it. This is, um...important intel on the enemy. In order to know the enemy—"

"This boy is younger than you, is he not?!"

"That isn't what you should be focusing on!"

Alice's deflection was in vain. The queen's eyes were glued to the screen.

"You had such a tender boy undress and... No. I suppose a boy of this age does have a certain captivating beauty about him, like a large flower on the cusp of blooming."

"......Come again?"

"His sunbaked skin perfectly captures the aura of a youth in his prime. And the prominence of his muscles along his neck is beautiful. And oh, those drenched black locks. Why, the way the ends of his hair cling to his neck and flick slightly could only be described as precious..."

"...Um, Mother?"

"Nevertheless!" The queen lifted her head animatedly. She turned around vigorously enough to overwhelm her daughter. "Nevertheless, Alice! A princess must have incredible self-control. I cannot believe you would do something so shameless as to disgrace this boy. Most of all, as your mother, I would like you to learn the charm of a mature man!"

"Mother! As I said, I am not engaging in any disgraceful activity!" Alice retorted, red in the face. "I am observing the enemy. I look at this every night to see his bare...no, I mean, to understand him better. I never renege on my daily study of—"

"Every night?!"

"That wasn't the point!"

She was too slow.

This black-haired boy was a stranger to the queen. She could only assume her own daughter had been watching him unconscionably night after night.

"I am confiscating this."

"Nooooo!"

"Oh...wait, Alice? Stop that! Let go!"

Alice was feverishly intent on stopping the queen from taking away the screen.

INTERMISSION

The Center of This World

Who is the supreme authority of this Empire?

If you posed this question to any citizen, Imperial or otherwise, they would all surely agree: the Imperial assembly.

They were the powerful, the pundits, and the wealthy chosen by the nation at large. The decisions of these select few lawmakers determined everything in the Empire.

However...

There was one unwritten, ultimate rule that every Imperial assembly member was aware of: They would never oppose the Eight Great Apostles, the eight people endowed with supreme authority who led the ruling body.

Few citizens in the Empire or otherwise had learned that these were the people who were truly at its helm. In fact, the existence of the Eight Great Apostles itself was a secret. The only ones who knew of them were the Imperial assembly members and the soldiers of the Imperial forces. That was exactly what made the Eight Great Apostles the supreme authority.

"But that's not true—not at all."

Klack...klack... The sound of hard heels echoed as they hit the ground, superimposed by her voice.

"I'm not sure whether to call it downright mystifying or plain insane. The Imperial citizens, citizens of other countries, the higher-ups, and even the Imperial assembly—none of them understands. No, perhaps they've simply forgotten?"

A tall, rather intelligent-looking military woman wearing becoming black-rimmed glasses strode down the hallway.

Risya In Empire.

A genius who had climbed her way to the fifth seat of the Saint Disciples, the strongest military force in the Empire, at just twenty-two years of age.

"But really, everyone should be aware. Of the greatest of them all."

She progressed down the corridor bathed in vermilion.

"None but the Lord stands at the pinnacle of the world."

The Lord, Yunmelngen.

Both the symbol of the Empire and the one and only master Risya served. It was they who truly helmed the Empire. And yet, the Lord had not made a move.

They lived in seclusion within the windowless building called the Castle Tower Seat. They never exercised their authority. That was why the people had temporarily forgotten who truly held supreme authority.

"They are so thoughtless, after all. Had the Lord not exercised their authority over the Eight Great Apostles, the Empire would have started an all-out war with the Sovereignty."

She continued down the glass passage to the topmost floor of the four buildings, the Heaven Between Insight and Nosight. When she set foot in that place, the pungent scent of grass tickled Risya's nose.

"Your Excellency."

"_____"

Beyond the curtain that hung from the ceiling, the Lord's shadow wavered, as though illuminated by a candle.

"I have a suggestion. Why don't you exchange these tatami mats, or whatever you call them, with a wooden floor? The smell of grass is so strong, my nose wrinkles from the stench."

"Sure. We'll take the funds directly from your salary."

The curtain quickly opened to reveal…

…a silver beast chuckling.

The beast's entire body was covered in fox-like fur. However, their face was a cross between that of a cat and a human girl…or one might liken it to that. Their eyes were as large as a kitten's, and their features would make any human fall in love at first sight. Even the sharp canines peeking from the corner of the beast's mouth were charming.

That very beast sat in a chair, legs crossed, head propped in their hand.

A beastperson. A living being who existed only in the likes of fairy tales.

"You are early, Risya."

"Well, Your Excellency, you would be just as mystified if I turned up late. You'd tell me I've made your boredom exponentially worse."

"Hmm? I am not so petty." Lord Yunmelngen's voice was buoyant. **"So, what has brought you here?"**

"The matter that concerned you, Your Excellency."

"And what was that?"

"It seems the Successor of the Black Steel has returned. Surely you remember that Unit 907 has been outside the Empire for some time. Now, where were they again…?"

Risya spread open a paper memo. She glanced at the map printed on it.

"Yes, it appears they're in the far-east Altoria district. There's a record of them presenting their military IDs when they passed through the border checkpoint."

They were far from the Imperial capital. Their return would take several days, even along the shortest route.

"…That's a problem," the silver-haired beastperson lamented from atop their chair. "**Those astral swords are precious, after all. He's putting us in a bind by taking them out willy-nilly. I suppose Crow never told him that.**"

"Crow… Oh, him. What a nostalgic name."

Crossweil Nes Lebeaxgate.

At one time, he had been the leader of the Saint Disciples, the Lord's right hand.

"I heard that he was Iska's teacher, but I do wonder where he is and what he could be up to now. The vagabond."

"**I do not. He can do as he likes.**"

The silver-haired beastperson yawned deeply. A conspicuously inhuman row of sharp teeth peeked from their mouth.

"**Risya, please call the Successor of the Black Steel here.**"

"Oh. So that must mean…"

"**It is time. I will instruct him about the astral swords starting from the ground up in place of that bungling teacher.**"

"You are sure about that?"

Risya narrowed her eyes from behind her glasses.

The astral swords. What had the so-called Astrals been calculating when they had forged those instruments?

Iska had not been told the truth. At best, he would know only that his master had bequeathed them to him under peculiar circumstances.

"I'm sure that will make the Eight Great Apostles sweat."

"**Such is my aim. I think they will show their faults if I begin to act… Hwaaah.**" Then the beastperson yawned once again. "**Oh, I've stayed up for two whole hours. Time to go back to bed.**"

"Yes, yes. Then I will wake you when Unit 907 returns to the Imperial capital. They're still in the far-eastern reaches of Altoria, so I'm sure it will be some time."

"...Risya, what did you just say?"

"Excuse me?"

Risya, who had turned away from the Lord, whipped around upon being addressed.

They were right before her eyes.

When had they moved? The silver-haired beastperson who had been sitting on a chair on a platform now stood atop the tatami mat, back stooped like a cat and gazing at Risya.

"Altoria? The far east? Did you say Altoria?"

"Yes, that is what I just said— Oh."

The Lord quickly snatched the paper from Risya's hand as nimbly as a fox or cat leaping at its prey.

"...Altoria."

"What is it, Your Excellency? I'm sure you have no need for that map, as you should know its contents already."

"I have changed my mind."

Lord Yunmelngen laughed. The beastperson crumpled the paper between humanlike hands.

"A memorable name. Risya, make preparations immediately."

"What could you possibly mean by that?"

"We will go. You and me both."

"What?! Wait, please, Your Excellency! I have an important meeting with the commanding officer of HQ after this. And I need to get ready for a press conference after that!"

"Oh? 'None but the Lord stands at the pinnacle of the world.' Which means my word is final. Was it not you who said this, Risya?"

"...So you were listening."

She nodded reluctantly as the beastperson pulled her along.

The Lord had thoroughly exasperated her.

CHAPTER 4

The Forbidden, Forgotten Name

1

Imperial territory. Easternmost Altoria jurisdiction.

Center of the eastern edge of the Empire, Altoria City.

"Is this an industrialized area?"

"It is what it looks like."

Jhin had said that to Rin, who was murmuring while looking out the window of the large car.

"There's plenty of land in the countryside. The outskirts are for dairy pasture, and they use this area for industry, apparently. They collect the iron ore from all over the Empire here."

"…So it's a military operation?"

"Why would something as large as that be out here? They make cars and airplanes, at most."

Manufacturing plants dotted the vast green plains. Wisps of white smoke rose from the chimneys post-filtering.

"Hey, Iska?" Commander Mismis leaned out the car window. "I still don't see the place Miss Sisbell was taken yet."

"...It's not going to *look* like there's anything shady going on there, duh."

They were seeing only one large factory after the other. Though all the buildings were easily large enough for hiding a single person, just as Jhin had pointed out, they were mostly plane and car factories, and privately owned at that.

...The workers who aren't in on it at the factories would create a huge commotion if they discovered Sisbell.

...So they wouldn't be able to use a facility unless it had ties to the Hydra.

That was likely why Rin also felt dubious.

It would have been easier for them to take Sisbell to a cheap hotel in an out-of-the-way town or keep her confined in a rented warehouse rather than in an industrial area like this.

Why would they bring her here?

"Well, whatever. We're going to where the signal came from, at any rate. Then we can talk after."

Rin held an earring in the image of a sun. They had come here believing that the transmission from the IC card hidden inside it pointed to the location where Sisbell was being held. They couldn't turn back now.

"The coordinates are close. Do you see anything suspicious, Imperial swordsman?"

"Nope, not at all." Iska was also paying close attention. Just as Rin had pointed out, no matter how far they drove, the only buildings intermittently popping up across the vast plain were factories. "Just the same old landscape."

"Keep your eyes peeled. I'm sure *you'd* be able to see through a concrete wall with your naked eyes."

"What are you going on about this time...?"

"I bet you could track Lady Sisbell's scent if it was coming downwind."

"What do you think I am?!"

He opened the map with chagrin.

"A suspicious-looking location, though...," Iska mused. "If we can tell that the place is fishy at a glance, then I think the locals would see it that way, too."

"Iska." Nene, who was in the driver's seat, pointed up ahead. "The coordinates are over there."

She gestured to a construction building partitioned by concrete walls. They were still too far away from it to get a clear look at what was going on there.

"Nene, could you do a loop around the wall?"

"You got it, Commander. They'll suspect us if I slow down, so I'll keep the same speed."

They headed to the factory where the coordinates seemed to lead them. As the car approached, the scenery came into focus.

"Hey, what's going on here...?" Jhin leaned forward. "This isn't a manufacturing plant. It's just ruins."

The dingy wall had been buffeted by wind and rain for years, leaving it in shambles. The overgrown thicket of wild grasses had grown taller than Iska, blocking the entrance to the grounds.

Both what remained of the factory and the concrete wall around it were dilapidated. No light shone from inside the building's broken windowpanes, and it didn't seem like it would have electricity or running water. Just as Jhin had proclaimed, it seemed that all production had ceased, leaving only ruins.

"...Looks like it could be haunted," Commander Mismis remarked.

"...Haunted? I'd be more concerned about the rats that are probably infesting the place, Commander. I bet there are a ton of cobwebs all over the ceiling. Yikes! I can't handle stuff like this...," Nene replied.

It seemed to be deserted. If Sisbell was confined here, they could understand why no one had spotted her.

However...

Was this really where she was being held?

…If they had Sisbell, there would be soldiers on guard and security cameras set up.

…But I don't see anything like that.

Perhaps they had foregone the guards to really sell that the place was abandoned and deceive any pursuers. But a strategy like that would be too much of a gamble for the Hydra. The chances they wouldn't assign someone to keep watch over Sisbell were slim to none.

Maybe this wasn't the place? As Iska hesitated over vocalizing his doubts, someone else did it for him.

"Now that I think about it, this is futile." Rin, who had been silent until then, suddenly opened the car door…while it was still traveling down the road. "Nene, or whoever you are, stop the car. If there isn't surveillance, then you should be able to park by the wall without issue."

"Whoa?! W-wait a second, Miss Rin. I'll stop—just calm down!"

The vehicle came to an abrupt halt. That same instant, Rin leaped out of it. She stared intently at the dilapidated factory from a giant hole in the concrete wall.

"I don't see any indication of surveillance cameras. If there had been some, then we could have been sure this was it. Then the only way to find out is to enter the grounds… So, Commander."

"Y-yes?"

Rin shrugged at Commander Mismis, who was also staring up at the factory.

"What do we do in this situation?" Rin asked.

"…What do you mean?"

"Our agreement was that you would take me to Lady Sisbell's location. We made a mutual agreement not to interfere with each other thereafter, but as you can see, there is no proof of Lady Sisbell being here."

"…Oh. You're right." Commander Mismis crossed her arms.

She gazed out into thin air for a while as though she was in thought. "So you mean you'd like us to search this factory? Um, hmm…I'm not so sure…"

"We will make an additional trade. I will give you something of value as well."

Rin pulled out skin-colored self-adhesives from the handbag she had left in the car. They were likely from the same supply of backups she had given to Commander Mismis while crossing the Imperial checkpoint. There were five in total.

She pushed them into Mismis's chest.

"You may have all the self-adhesives I have on me. I am sure you have some from Lady Sisbell, but as I told you the day before, those will not match your skin tone."

"Uh…!"

"I'm sure you have no qualms."

"Commander! Iska, Jhin, over here!" someone called from a ways off. Nene, who had followed the wall and walked farther away, motioned for them to come closer.

"Something's up with this building," she told them. "Could we have time to search it? Even an hour?"

"What's suddenly gotten into you, Nene…?!"

"This," she replied.

It was the giant concrete wall that surrounded the grounds. Nene pointed at double doors that seemed to be the entrance. Beside them was an engraved metal sign that read:

OMEN INSTITUTE FOR ASTRAL RESEARCH, ALTORIA BRANCH.

"Huh? That's where we are?" Iska couldn't believe his eyes.

Omen, collective of geniuses. In the Empire, where research on astral power was taboo, this organization alone was formally permitted to do their research. And if this place had that moniker, then that meant…

"So it was a research facility initially, not a factory..."

If this was an Omen establishment, then it was one of the country's great secrets. Only those related to the organization would have been allowed to set foot in it. Even Iska, an Imperial soldier, had never entered an Omen building before.

"......Ngh. It is, but...," Nene mumbled. She looked between the rusted sign and the virtually ruined grounds. "I'm curious. Commander, I'd like to explore this place a little!"

"Excuse me? W-wait, Nene! You can't waltz on in to Omen property. The front doors are shut!"

"Over here."

Nene pointed at the wall. Years of exposure to the elements had worn it down and caused the concrete to crumble. There was even a hole that was large enough for Iska and Jhin to enter.

"In we go... Hmm. I think I can get through. Miss Rin should be able to fit, and Iska and Jhin are both thin, so you two should be able to as well," Nene said. "I think if anyone gets stuck, it'll be the commander, considering her boobs and backside."

"What are you implying, Nene?!"

"C'mon, boss! You're holding us up."

"D-don't push me, Jhin!"

The commander, Jhin, and Rin headed through the hole after Nene.

"You too, Iska!"

"All right, I'm coming."

He looked around again. The car was in the shadow of the wall. Even the few vehicles passing by on the road made no sign of coming closer to them. Once he made sure of that, Iska also leaped through the opening.

On the other side was a branch of the Omen Institute for Astral Research.

Iska found the abandoned grounds even quieter than they'd seemed from outside the wall.

The site was overgrown. A single decommissioned car stood in the parking lot, its tires deflated. In one section, heaps of unrecognizable equipment were piled in the garbage area.

"Uhhh...this place actually seems creepy. It's really run-down..."

"The research center itself is amazing, Commander."

It was a three-story institution. Even from a distance, they could tell that the windowpanes were all broken. From up close, the concrete cracks seemed almost like spiderwebs. Moss and unidentified black bugs crawled along the walls, giving the place an ominous aura.

"Hmm......"

One of them looked up with glistening eyes.

"Nene, did you find something?"

"No, nothing." She shook her head, long red hair whipping around in its ponytail. "It's actually very interesting that there's nothing here."

"Huh?"

"Not a single trace of astral energy."

Klonk. Nene knocked on the concrete wall with her fist.

"If this used to be an astral power research institute, it'd be a problem if any astral energy leaked out, right? So they should have astral energy detectors outside the building and along the inner part of the walls, too. It's weird they don't."

"Don't you think they might have removed them when they closed down, Nene?"

"I considered that, but..." She pointed at the parking lot and the garbage area. "They've left a car and their machinery. I doubt they would carefully remove the detectors and leave everything else."

"Oh...right."

"Also, Miss Rin, may I ask you a question?" Next, Nene gestured toward the wall of the edifice. "So astral power research institutes should have a duct to pump astral energy up from the ground, right? With a slightly specialized filter on it."

"Uh?! How did you…?!"

"I saw one at Snow and Sun."

"…………"

Now it was Rin's turn to fall silent.

"They probably process the astral energy they pump up from the ground outdoors in some way, right? They select only the energy they want to study, then pipe it into the building. That's why I'm convinced the walls should have the same kind of tubing on them."

"…That's exactly correct." Atypically, a strained smile graced Rin's face. "The astral energy that surges from a vortex is never just of one type. You would need a classifier to sort them… Though I cannot go into details, I also had the same reservations."

"I knew it."

"Mm-hmm. I recognize this is rude; however, I will say that I underestimated you, Nene. It never crossed my mind that you could have been so observant at Snow and Sun…" Rin crossed her arms and turned to Mismis. "There you have it, Commander."

"What?! Uh, ummm… Oh, I get that much; it's okay. Even I understand."

"This research lab is a sham. They probably made it just to resemble an astral power research institute."

"Why did you beat me to it, Jhin?!" Mismis exclaimed.

"The sun is setting. C'mon, we're going, boss." He had a case over his shoulder. Jhin pulled out the sniper rifle stored in it and threw the case to the side. "We've got to act like Imperial soldiers occasionally."

"What? Then that means…"

"If this is an illegal research lab, then this is an undeniable breach of the law. Not like I could keep silent as an Imperial soldier."

Yes. At that moment, the situation underwent a complete about-face for Unit 907.

...If this had been an Imperial lab, we wouldn't have been able to intervene.

...But if this is an illegal research facility, on the other hand, then the circumstances are completely reversed. As members of the Imperial army, we're obligated to intervene.

They now had a reason to get on board. Instead of retrieving Sisbell, their objective was to investigate who had illegally constructed the lab.

"That's how it is." He winked at Rin, who was silently standing by. "Change of plans. We're going with you."

"As you wish." Rin cracked her neck. "I've been building up a lot of stress these past few days. Since it's not an Imperial facility, you won't mind if I let off some steam, will you?"

The Empire. Visgehten, capital of the fourth state.

This was where the one and only "unburied" vortex within the Empire had been preserved.

Astral power was originally taboo. Though the Imperial forces had destroyed all the vortices the Empire discovered, here in this province, one remained scrupulously preserved under the auspices of Omen, collective of geniuses.

All the information related to astral power that existed within the Empire rested here.

"Hey there, Nameless. How are you doing today?"

"You asked me that three hours ago."

"It seems you are cognizant, then. We have been inspecting your arm within this specialized astral power private room for three hours, after all."

The examination room was filled with bluish-white light. A jubilant voice and the sound of footsteps echoed against the room's opal tiles.

"Michaela, the chart, if you could?"

"Chief Newton."

"What is it?"

"You already have it in your hand."

"Oh my. It seems you're right. I was so lost in thought, I'd forgotten about it. Like when you're looking for your glasses while they're on your face."

When the female medical officer dressed in office attire pointed that out, the mustachioed chief smiled wanly.

Saint Disciple of the tenth seat and head of the laboratory, Sir Karosos Newton.

His nickname was the "sickliest researcher." The man's shoulders and limbs looked as though they would snap against the slightest of breezes. They betrayed the fact he was an exception—a civilian among the members of the world's greatest military force, the Saint Disciples.

He waved a hand at his colleague, who sat on a bed.

"So. I'll ask again. How do you feel, Nameless?"

"............"

There was something unusual about the other man's appearance. He was clothed in a dark-gray coat suit from head to toe. His face was hidden, and it was unlikely anyone could even put a stethoscope to his chest. He didn't look like a patient undergoing an examination at all.

"...*My wounds sting.*"

Nameless. The eighth seat of the Saint Disciples attempted to lift his exposed, muscular right arm. It barely moved an inch. He lifted his shoulder ever so slightly, but that was all he could manage. Manipulating his hands or fingers was beyond him.

"The plan to capture the queen. Growley, some old-timer who heads the Zoa household, flooded me with astral power, and this is the result. How many times must I explain?"

His right limb was covered in deep-purple bruises.

Though they looked like burns, in actuality, they were the symptoms of a corrosive astral power illness produced by the Vice astral power.

"I am Growley, the head of the Zoa. Now, how about we weigh out your sins?"

"These are avatars. You're already guilty of a crime. That crime has become your punishment."

Nameless still hadn't realized the full extent of the astral power, even at the end of the incident. The astral energy had materialized as avatar beasts he'd clashed with, but when they attacked him, his right arm became immobilized. That was all he knew.

"Astral power illness comes in an infinite number of varieties, after all." Chief Newton looked at the chart, his voice buoyant as he read it, almost as though he was enjoying this. "You fought a purebred, yes? There's not much we can do if the Empire's knowledge of astral power illness and how to treat it doesn't work in this case. Goes to show how terrible the monster you faced was."

"Enough chitchat."

The Saint Disciple of the eighth seat glared at the researcher.

"What will happen to my arm? Will it rot away at this rate?"

"Perhaps. Or perhaps not. The quickest method of dealing with it would be to cut off your right shoulder and to replace it with an artificial limb like your left."

"Works for me."

It was as simple as that. As Nameless urged them to chop off his limb, Michaela shivered and paled. Wasn't he at least hesitant?

This wasn't just any arm. This was the arm of the Empire's greatest assassin. It was worth more than one of the nation's most treasured swords. Why didn't he even feel the fear of losing it?

"No reason to be so hasty." Chief Newton tossed aside the chart and shrugged. "According to your report, that Vice astral power, or whatever it's called, flinched at the anti–astral power grenade, right? In that case, there's a high likelihood we'll be able to eliminate it."

"_____"

"We have resources astral power is averse to. Of particular note is the ore we collected from the highly contaminated region of Katalisk, which we can dissolve into a medicine. Michaela, please make arrangements immediately. Vary the concentration and try to collect as much of a sample as you can."

"I can hear the thrill in your voice."

Nameless sighed.

To this emaciated scientist, even his astral power illness was nothing but precious research. He was devoid of the pride physicians took in healing patients.

"You can use my body as a sample, but don't think that I'll let you toy with me without consequences if you're not able to cure me in the end."

"I will do all in my power to cure you. I have never treated a patient with astral power illness lightly." Chief Newton turned to the physician behind him and winked. "Isn't that right, Michaela?"

"That was creepy."

"Apparently, the trick to winking is practice. Now, that aside, I do consider myself an outstanding researcher, despite appearances. I won't deny that there are incredibly rare cases of those you would call mad scientists in the world, though."

"Now that you mention it…"

He laughed in a low growl. As he sat on the bed, Nameless's shoulders quivered from mirth.

"I know of one. A certain someone who was taken under another's

wing but who secretly proceeded with research that outpaced even Omen's morals. Someone who started doing human experimentation. Apparently, she was also a pretty decent mad scientist herself."

"............" Chief Newton went silent. He stroked his beloved beard as his face, unusually for him, clouded when Nameless pointed that out. "...All I can say is that it was a disappointment. That was what she was."

"What was her name?"

"Kelvina. She had the potential to become the best astral power illness researcher here at Omen. She was outstanding when it came to experimentation—that's for sure." Chief Newton looked up at the ceiling. "But she had no morals and crossed a line indulging in her intellectual curiosity. She went so far as to remodel her own home into a laboratory so she could conduct human experiments without batting an eye. By the time I got there, it was too late..."

"Wasn't she arrested for treason?"

"She escaped."

"...What?"

A slight amount of apprehension entered Nameless's voice. The Saint Disciple, who hadn't so much as flinched at the prospect of having his limb cut off, had changed his tune when Chief Newton revealed that.

"You mean she escaped from the Divine Gallows?"

"I suppose she did."

"............"

That was the most strictly monitored jail in the Empire, which held only the mightiest witches and sorcerers, along with Imperial traitors.

"Fugitive Zero. I think that's the catchy nickname they gave her. Perhaps the ninth seat guarding her made a blunder?"

"It was not Statulle's oversight. And if I may add one more thing, I highly doubt she escaped through her own abilities."

"...You think there's a mole?"

"Very likely. And it must be someone with quite a bit of influence over the higher-ups in the Imperial forces."

He sighed. The man in the white coat exhaled very, very deeply.

"Remember this? About a year ago, one of our own colleagues, a former Saint Disciple, broke a witch out of the jail. His name was, um… Michaela?"

"It was Iska."

"That's right. But this is a different situation than what happened then. For starters, Iska didn't bust into the Divine Gallows, and most importantly, he was caught afterward."

Even a Saint Disciple wouldn't have been able to accomplish that feat. Regardless of whether you could disable the Empire's security system temporarily and devise a break-in, the perpetrator would eventually be apprehended.

"However, they still have not found the person who broke out Kelvina. So how did they open the locks to the Divine Gallows? How did they get her out…?"

"*Or, better yet, why did they break her out?*"

"That's the question. I still have no answer as to why they would want to free a woman as dangerous as her— Oh my. Seems we've made quite a divergence from the original conversation." Chief Newton looked up at the clock on the wall and scratched the back of his head. "Let's make arrangements for the treatment. I'll come back in seven hours next time. Make sure to get some rest until then."

"*Understood.*"

"Keep in mind that patients live longer when they follow their doctor's orders. Now then, I bid you adieu."

His white coat flipped around as he left the examination room. In the hallway…

"……Kelvina, then," he murmured in a voice so stifled, even the woman walking beside him wouldn't be able to hear. "Kelvina Sofita Elmos. What a repugnant name I've remembered."

2

Imperial territory. Birthplace of Witches.

A small, dusty room.

The ceiling was covered in cobwebs. Unfamiliar bugs crawled out of the fissures in the concrete.

"............"

"Don't glare at me like that, Princess Sisbell. I'm just bad at cleaning. This is what my room normally looks like." The researcher—a woman with red hair—laughed mirthfully. "Or do you mean to tell me that you take issue with how I've received a princess? Would you like me to hurry up and take off your shackles?"

"No." Still bound faceup on the dusty bed, Sisbell glared at the woman looking down on her.

The researcher's skin was ashen, as though she was malnourished. She had bags under her eyes from lack of sleep. Though she looked incredibly ill, her eyes lit up as she gazed at Sisbell's face.

"...Kelvina, or whatever your name is. It's your eyes. I do not appreciate the way you look down on me."

"Ha-ha. What an adorable witch you are."

Kelvina Sofita Elmos. The odd woman swooped the white coat she wore to reveal rows of syringes along the wall.

"Hng!"

"Oh, but you cried and shouted the first time you saw these. *Stop it, stop it!* you said. Are you really that scared of needles?"

"......Yes. I remember that quite well." Sisbell bit her lip from where she was still lying down. She could hardly hold back her fear and humiliation. "Because you suctioned the tears I shed with a syringe and called it *precious witch bodily fluid*. That made me shudder."

Sisbell didn't sense any animosity or hostility from the woman.

It was the first time she had experienced it—the fear of running up against someone's bottomless curiosity.

…She only thinks of witches as research samples.

…This is the first time I've met an Imperial with such little humanity.

Though the Empire's discrimination of witches disgusted her, this woman went beyond that. She was possessed by desires of an unknown nature.

"Now, don't worry. We won't be using the agents in these syringes for some time." Kelvina lovingly stroked one of the instruments with an even gentler touch than she'd used when examining Sisbell. "It's still time to be patient. Your donor said I wasn't to lay hands on you. Your astral power seems quite valuable."

"…Is your donor Lord Talisman?"

"Oh, so you knew? Yes, it was indeed that sorcerer."

She didn't even attempt to conceal who was behind it. And even though he was her coconspirator, she'd still called him a sorcerer.

"Do you really despise the Sovereignty that much?"

"Hmm? No, not in the slightest," Kelvina said. "I don't hate the Nebulis Sovereignty at all."

She ruffled her dull red hair. She didn't have any makeup on.

"Unlike the people at the Imperial headquarters, I don't want to exterminate witches and sorcerers. That would be a waste. You all are far too precious research samples for that."

"…So you don't think of us as human?"

"As human? Now, how would you categorize that?"

"What?"

"There are only two types of things in this world: research samples and everything else. I don't care whether you're human."

Kelvina stared directly into Sisbell's face. Her pale lips formed something that resembled a slight smile.

"You witches are the former, and the Imperials walking about are the latter. So you should be happy. In my world, you're valuable."

"............"

Kelvina looked into her eyes. Their noses were nearly touching. Sisbell silently closed her eyes at this mad scientist, who was ogling her without so much as blinking.

Sisbell didn't want to see her. She'd had enough close-ups of this woman's face.

"...You are an aberration," Sisbell hissed.

"Very good," the woman replied.

"Huh!"

She felt something on her chest. Her eyes still shut, Sisbell tried to resist as she was groped. Though technically, it was actually her astral crest that Kelvina was touching.

"That's what everyone who envies my genius calls me. Omen, the Imperial headquarters, they all say it. *You're wrong*. Isn't that amusing? In the end, the only people who knew my true worth were the Eight Great Apostles."

"What?"

"...Oh, I've said too much. Mustn't do that. I haven't spoken to anyone but myself for some time. I'm practically drunk on conversation."

The princess opened her eyes. Kelvina had covered her mouth in an almost childlike manner. Though Sisbell was curious about the Eight Great Apostles, in this situation, inquiring about that would likely be futile.

"What's your aim?" she asked instead.

"My aim? Why, nothing but uncovering the truth of this world through research. For I am a scientist."

It was such a respectable goal that it felt almost anticlimactic. But any of Sisbell's presumptions were quickly blown away by what the woman said next.

"My greatest interest is the depths of the planet."

Sisbell inhaled sharply.

"Princess Sisbell, do you know what dwells there?"

"......?" She paused upon being questioned.

The depths of the planet? What did that mean? No matter how far down you dug, the only thing you'd find in the lowest strata of the earth was bedrock.

However...

Sisbell recalled the face of Talisman, head of the Hydra. She was certain the man who had snuck into the Lou villa had said something along those lines...

"We require the Empire's power to reach the planet's core."

"Let's join hands, Sisbell. The astral power in you can reveal the secrets of this planet. I would like you to work for me in the future."

"...That's something I would like to know as well."

She gritted her teeth.

Sisbell shouted at the researcher looking down on her, "This planet's core? Just what are you all hiding?!"

CHAPTER 5

The Taboo of the Planet

The Omen Institute for Astral Research. A fake building.

The field grasses on the grounds had grown into a forest, and the paint on the walls was peeling from exposure. Perhaps the premises had been abandoned long ago. Or perhaps its dilapidated appearance was the product of deliberate design. Until they entered the lab, they couldn't be sure.

"...It's locked, of course." Jhin kicked the front entrance.

Without any electricity to power the infrared sensors on the doors, the entrance was practically just a heap of steel. They would have a hell of a time forcing the doors open through sheer manpower alone.

"Opening the front doors is the easiest way in, though. Nene, you don't happen to have a bomb on you, do you? Like one disguised as an earring or something?"

"No, I left it at home."

"Wait, you seriously have something like that? Nah, never mind. Looks like you're up, Iska. Can you open them?"

"...I don't think I *can't* cut through them, but..."

Iska eyed the incredibly heavy-looking doors up and down, then placed his hand on the grip of his astral sword. One swing wouldn't be enough. But if he slashed at them two or three times, he'd probably be able to create a small opening.

"Get back. I'll do it."

That had come from behind him. Rin was hunched over and running her fingertips through the dirt on the ground.

"You just need me to smash it to bits, yes? That's simple."

The ground swelled. The earth, which had taken on a viscous quality, gathered as though it had a will, shaping itself into a gigantic form as Rin rested on one knee in front of it. A golem emerged.

"Now, golem, smash that."

"Wait a sec!"

Just as Iska and the others managed to leap away, the golem launched its gigantic fist, blowing away the front doors of the building without a trace.

"You almost caught us in its punch!"

"You were simply too slow to clear the area... Hmph. I can't say I didn't expect it, but it seems the interior is in a similar state of disrepair."

She stared into the whirling dust and scowled.

The hallway was practically pitch-black. The scant illumination that was present came from the sunlight that had managed to stream through the shuttered windows. If they'd come here at night, exploring this place would have been out of the question.

"I'll go first. You may follow after me."

"What are you going to do with that golem? We can't have that giant thing coming with us—it'll get in the way."

"It will wait here. And..." In response to Jhin, Rin seemed to have remembered something. She headed back where she had stood, then placed her hand on the ground again. "I'll have a golem keep watch at the entrance to make sure no one will follow us. Plus one more. I suppose I'll give it a shield just to be safe."

The ground writhed. Instead of a golem, this time Rin's astral powers birthed a doll about as tall as Jhin. Though it was smaller and slenderer than the golem, the thing was all the quicker for it. This was an earth soldier.

"Walk one step behind me."

After receiving the order, the doll dutifully followed after Rin into the building.

The moment they set foot in the lab, Nene and Commander Mismis scowled. The stench of rust, dirt, and mildew assaulted them.

"...*Ahem...* Ugh, Nene, are you okay?"

"Ugh. My nose feels like it'll fall off. It smells terrible in here. I should have brought a mask with me."

Whenever they took a step forward, the dust billowed around them. It was thick as a carpet. They couldn't have guessed how many decades it could have taken for such a thick layer of the stuff to have built up.

"Based on the dust, it doesn't seem like they just made this place look like it was abandoned. The lights are completely out, too."

Jhin pulled out a communications device. He turned the brightness to its highest setting and used it in place of a flashlight to illuminate the ground.

"Oh, Jhin. I can hold the communications device."

"Hmm?"

"You wouldn't be able to use your gun if you're holding that. I can carry mine with one hand, but you've got a sniper rifle."

"You better not trip and drop it."

"I wouldn't! ...But it sure is dark here. Even a haunted house in an amusement park wouldn't be this poorly lit."

Commander Mismis gripped Jhin's communications device.

The floor was gray from all the dust. Across the ceiling, several tubes followed the walls and stretched into the back.

"So those astral energy pipes you mentioned earlier, Nene—," Mismis started to say.

"These are completely different. They look like they're for ventilation," Rin replied. She continued straight into the vast building, earth soldier still behind her. "I was too hasty. I should have prepared a dozen or so dolls for such a large edifice. I could have simplified our investigation had I ordered them to walk around."

Rin clicked her tongue. Earth astral mages had a few shortcomings. Unlike snow, ice, and flame astral powers, which could be created out of thin air, earth astral power could manipulate soil at most. Since there was no earth within the building, she wouldn't be able to craft more dolls.

"So be it. You all may continue to explore the first floor. I will go back and—"

"Wait, Rin."

"What is it, Imperial swordsman?"

"The dust cuts off."

"Wha—?!"

When Iska said that, Rin's eyes opened wide. She flipped around like a spinning top to glance at their surroundings. Though the filth hadn't disappeared entirely, the thick layer of dust caking the floor had indeed disappeared.

"Since when?"

"Since we turned that last corner. It petered out gradually, so I didn't catch it right away."

They looked farther ahead.

"If the floor is this clean, that's proof someone's been walking around here pretty often, right?"

"...Seems that way."

Rin began to move once again, keeping her footsteps as light as possible as she crept forward this time, as though she were trailing prey.

There was a glow. Rin squinted when she saw the light that streamed in ahead from a four-way corridor.

"It seems they've finally given themselves away. Though they've crafted this place to look like it's abandoned, it seems they do have electricity deeper in."

Those must have been the ceiling lamps. Rin slowly progressed down the dimly lit corridor toward the source of the illumination.

Klack…klack…

They heard footsteps from around the corner.

Who was it?

There was one set of footsteps. Someone was approaching Iska and the others from farther in as they hid in the shadows of the corridor.

"I'm going to capture them."

Rin reached into her skirt. She slipped out a small knife from the place she was storing who knows how many weapons of assassination.

"If there is only one, I will handle it. Two, and the doll will help. Anything more than three, and I will need to count on you."

Then she went silent.

Iska and the others did as well. They didn't so much as give a yes or no, simply nodding so as not to be heard.

Rin leaned forward so she could leap out at any time she needed. Behind her, Unit 907 stood at the ready to provide backup.

The footsteps grew closer.

Klack, klack… The sound echoed as the footfalls steadily grew louder. Whoever it was, they were about to reach the four-way intersection. They saw the tips of someone's shoes around the corner. That moment, Rin reached out for the person's ankles, grabbing hold and wrenching them up.

"I caught them!"

"Yeek!" screamed a man hysterically as he fell over. Rin straddled him before he could say anything and held the edge of her naked blade to his neck.

"…Eek?! Wh-what's going on?! Who the hell are you?!"

"Shush."

As she pressed the knife to his neck, Rin stared at him coldly.

The man was only in his teens and wearing civilian clothes. Though Rin was probably younger than he was, with her knife at his throat and her threatening tone, she was far more of a veteran than he was.

"Follow my orders. One, contacting your companions is forbidden."

"C-companions?!"

"Next up, weapons. The people behind me will now confiscate any you have. Do not resist."

"I haven't got any!"

"I see. So you won't be complying, then?"

"N-no! I actually...h-haven't done anything! Companions? I haven't got any, and I'm not packing any heat. You can tell by looking!"

"..."

Still straddling the man's chest, Rin glanced down at his civilian outfit.

He wore a thin shirt and jeans. She wouldn't even need to make him strip. He couldn't have hidden guns or blades under that getup.

"It seems you truly are unarmed."

"L-like I said—"

"Hey."

Jhin took a knee and leaned over the man, who was still lying faceup. He thrust his military ID at him.

"We're from the Imperial forces. We're temporarily putting you under arrest."

"Th-the forces?! What are you doing here...?!"

"We're doing a home search."

"...What did you just say?"

"We're looking for a woman in this place. She's a girl in her mid-teens with long strawberry-blond hair. Anybody come to mind?"

"I-I've never seen anybody like her!"

He looked at Jhin and Rin fearfully, then at Iska and Commander Mismis. It didn't look like an act. He really seemed to be a civilian who was bewildered that the Imperial forces were interrogating him.

"Different question." Rin butted in again. "You do understand this establishment has been closed down, right?"

"What?"

"...Well, if you're going to feign ignorance..."

"I-I'm not! Wait, you've got me mixed up with someone else. I don't know. I'm just a part-timer!"

A part-timer? When the man said that, Iska and the others went silent and scowled.

...He doesn't even know this place was abandoned?

...But the front doors were closed.

What was going on?

"W-well, I did know that this place kind of looked like it was deserted. But that's all I've got. All I've been hired to do is clean the first floor and transfer the drugs once a week..."

"What drugs?"

"L-like I said, I don't— Ow?!"

"Be more discriminating with the words you use, Imperial."

She shaved off a thin layer of his skin, scraping the edge of her knife faintly across his neck. The restrained man screamed.

"Do you understand who is in charge here?"

"............"

"And your answer?" she pressed.

"I'm sorry..." The part-time worker turned pale and shuddered. "L-like I said, someone hired me. I'm telling you, all I do is change out the empty bottles and flasks in this creepy place!"

"Who hired you?"

"A redheaded lady. I don't know her name... She was tall for a woman and kind of talked like a guy...but I only speak to her when she pays me."

"You say you know nothing?"

"...Y-yes."

"..."

He was clueless.

Rin glared down at the man as he kept on insisting that and ground her molars in irritation. He didn't know where Sisbell was. This guy was a nobody. Just a local.

"I got it. In that case, show us where you transfer the drugs. After you do that, we'll be done with you."

"W-will you let me go then?!"

"Only if you follow orders. Get up."

Rin had pulled out a steel wire. She bound the man's wrists with it like handcuffs and pushed her knife to his back.

"Ouch!"

"Start walking forward. If you stop, I stab. If you scream, I stab. You do anything I find suspect, I stab. And if I'm feeling irritated, I might gore you just for the hell of it."

"That's ridiculous!"

"Take us to the woman if you want to live."

"...R-right away."

The man started walking quickly.

They proceeded down the lit hallway toward a door that was slightly ajar, which led to a pharmacy.

"So this is where you're working?"

"...Y-yes. Once a month, a ton of these weird metal cases are delivered, and I store them in here. The air-conditioning only works in this room."

Metal cases lined the walls of the area.

They were all locked up tight.

...I wonder what's inside. They aren't labeled.

...Maybe I could cut through the lid and take a peek? No, that would take too much time.

Iska estimated there were more than two hundred cases here. There was a faster way to do this than checking all of them.

"Rin."

"I know. We can simply ask the redheaded woman what's in all these containers. And where Lady Sisbell is. Hey, you."

"Y-yes?!"

"We know enough about the drug deliveries. Show us where the woman who hired you is."

"Here! This is where we meet!"

"What? What are you—? Tsk."

She didn't get to finish her sentence. Rin stopped speaking midway and shut her mouth.

It was below her feet. Right where she was standing, Rin could make out lines just the tiniest hair wide in the floor.

"A hidden door!"

It was an underground entrance. The establishment was large. If they hadn't gotten the man to squeal about the place, there was no way they would have found it.

"Give us the key."

"I—I don't have it. I don't open it. When we're supposed to transfer the goods, she unfastens it from underground."

"I see."

Thump... Rin poked the man in the back with her finger.

She was telling him to scram.

"We're done with you. You're free to do as you please."

"......Huh? Um, my hands are still bound."

"You can go call for help all you'd like outside the building. There's a chance you might betray us, so I'm not planning on freeing your hands. Or—"

"I'm sorry!"

The man didn't even look back as he bolted out the dimly lit corridor.

"Let's continue our search. Any objections, Commander Mismis?"

"N-no...but I wonder how we'll open this door."

"That's what they're for."

The earth doll burst.

The clod of soil in human form smoothly transformed into tiny particles of sand, sneaking into the incredibly thin crevices in the floor.

Kreak—the dull sound of metal being bent out of shape rang from under the floor. Immediately after that, the hidden door that had been fastened tight swung open as though a spring was being let loose.

"Whoa! That's amazing!" Nene's eyes glittered. "Miss Rin, how did you do that just now?"

"I had the doll enter the keyhole and destroy it. I would have had to give up if it was a password padlock mechanism, but a simple cylinder lock is easy enough to break."

"...Astral power sure is useful."

"I don't know about that. The only reason this worked is because I have the Earth astral power. Most are flame or wind or snow and are self-summoning types. My powers, on the other hand, are a manipulation type that can only take advantage of pre-existing soil. Putting it another way, such detailed—"

She stopped suddenly. Rin came back to her senses when she saw Nene had started writing notes.

"...Forget it. That's enough about me."

"Miss Rin, are you one of those people who usually keeps quiet but then can't stop talking once she gets going?"

"Sh-shut up! We've gotta go!"

Leading the earth doll along, Rin pointed at the hidden stairs.

They headed down. After they'd taken about twelve steps, a different variety of light started to filter in. It was a pale azure color. Using the light, which was almost the hue of the clear blue sea, as a waypoint, they made it to the bottom of the passageway. And ahead of them...

"...What is that?"

"Huh?! Wh-what the—?!"

Alarm marked Rin's and Commander Mismis's voices.

The light that filled the place was…

…dazzling astral energy.

It hadn't been shining down from the ceiling.

A giant machine furnace was set up in the large hall they arrived in. The faint bluish-green light poured from the furnace as though it were steam.

"Unbelievable… Is all of this coming from an astral energy reactor?!"

Rin took a step back against the nearly divine, brilliant light before her, almost as if she was overwhelmed.

"I thought there weren't any astral energy separation pipes. They couldn't have drawn this up from a vortex without putting it through a conversion process… Iska!" She balled her hands into fists and questioned him. "What is the meaning of this?! I thought you said astral power research was banned in the Empire? Ridiculous… What is this machine? Even the Sovereignty doesn't yet have the technology to harness energy directly from a vortex!"

"Do you really think I knew about this?"

"Guh."

"…To be frank, it even took me by surprise."

It wasn't as though Iska had been unreactive for no reason. He simply hadn't been able to say anything. This was just supposed to be a seemingly abandoned building where Sisbell was being held. He hadn't thought it would have been any more significant than that.

…But what is this place?

…What's going on with these machines?!

The hall was bathed with fantastical light, astral illumination flowing out from twenty furnaces. Each was of a slightly different hue.

There was flame, water, and wind. How many types of astral power had they collected here?

"Jhin."

"Don't ask me."

For once—a very rare occurrence—the silver-haired young man scowled ruefully.

"They went to the trouble of making this place look like it was abandoned, then hid the basement. This definitely isn't aboveboard Imperial research…"

"So the military isn't involved?"

"That I can't say. Underlings like us wouldn't know whether it's a national secret or if it never had to do with the forces in the first place, but…there's no way somebody got this together on their own just for kicks. Someone big has to be behind it all."

Prohibited astral power research.

If what Rin had said was true, then this facility was even more advanced than the ones in the Sovereignty.

…*The Imperial forces aren't involved. I want to believe that.*

…*I mean, no one ever told me about this place when I became a Saint Disciple!*

Just who could it be? Who was lurking in this hidden laboratory, and what were they researching?

"Hey, boss. Just to clear things up, did you know anything about this?" Nene asked Mismis.

"M-me?! I had no idea. Nene, do you have any idea what this furnace is?" she replied.

"…I have no idea." Nene readily shook her head. "I think this is a super-dangerous area. I don't think regular Imperial soldiers like us should have ever set foot in here."

"I actually think it makes sense." A bold smile formed over Rin's lips. She pushed farther into the hall with long strides, past the groaning furnaces. "I was wondering why they would have brought Lady Sisbell to these ruins, but now it makes sense. This seems like the perfect place for confining a captured astral mage."

The basement was hot and humid.

It was almost like a sauna. Just like the pitch-black floor aboveground, the hall here also had low visibility, though this time it was from all the vapor in the air.

"Rin, I don't think I need to tell you this, but be careful. This isn't any ordinary facility."

"You're a pain, Imperial swordsman. You think I would not be vigilant?"

Rin tossed her knife aside.

Then she pulled out a folding dagger from the pleats of her skirt and gripped it. It wasn't the kind you'd use for questioning. No, it was an assassination weapon that you could wield in battle to maim and kill with ease.

"…Who are you?"

Rin stopped in her tracks. There was a figure beyond the fog. But it wasn't moving in the slightest. Rin was sure her voice would have carried over to whoever it was.

"…Are they careless? They should be warier of trespassers." Her voice was cold. She readied the dagger and leaped.

"Wonderful! I don't know who you are, but I'll skewer you!" she shouted.

"W-wait, Rin! It's me!"

"Huh?! Lady Sisbell?!"

Rin quickly came to a halt. Iska, Jhin, Nene, and Commander Mismis did as well. But as they laid eyes on the girl, they couldn't believe what they were seeing. They hadn't expected to see something like this at all.

It was Sisbell, bound to a wheelchair.

Though she was trying to fight back her fear, it was plain to see on her charming face, even amid the fog. Her animated features were slightly flushed from excitement, and most importantly, they could not mistake the beauty of her beguiling strawberry-blond hair. This was Sisbell in the flesh.

"Rin!" the princess wailed. "Hurry, unbind me, please! Kelvina ran farther in!"

"...Kelvina?"

"The woman who's keeping me captive. She told me she had something she wanted me to see and brought me over. But when you showed up, she ran farther in!"

"Qu-quickly!"

Rin scrambled over. She cut the ropes binding Sisbell to the wheelchair one by one, then finally severed the bonds at Sisbell's hands.

"Phew. You are uninjured?" Rin seemed to calm as she watched Sisbell rise to her feet. "Good. This place is still shrouded in mystery, but Lady Alice and Her Majesty will both be relieved. You were so very lucky, Lady Sisbell. Especially since I was the one dispatched for you. Please do make sure you are grateful for that."

"Iska!"

"Yes, be grateful to Iska... Come again?"

She passed Rin by. For some reason, the sweet girl ran as fast as she could to Iska. Tears had begun to well in her eyes.

"Oh, I believed in you! I was not wrong to choose you. You are the perfect guard!"

"Uh...w-wait?!"

Sisbell grabbed him and wouldn't let go. She wrapped her arms around his back and squeezed, burying her face in his chest. In fact, he felt like she was intentionally pushing her chest into his.

"I was so, so anxious. Oh, how I've longed for the company of others. I was so lonesome...!"

"Uh, um, Sisbell?"

"Please never leave me again. Not for the rest of my life!"

"The rest of your life?!"

"Oh, is that Jhin there, too?"

Still latched onto Iska, Sisbell turned to the silver-haired young man.

"I also feel somewhat grateful to you, I suppose. Yes, as a reward for doing this, I shall add you to my personal guard starting today!"

"No thanks," he replied.

"It's the greatest honor you could have," Sisbell insisted.

"That just means nobody wants to do it."

"Wh-what are you trying to imply? As important as I am, I—"

It seemed she hadn't realized it. As she enthusiastically invited the two men into her guard, the women were glaring at her and looking incredibly disillusioned.

"...I went through so much." Nene sighed.

"...I just want to go home now."

"...Yeah. Maybe I'll pretend I never found her and just head back."

They were having second thoughts about rescuing her. And the next target of the women's gazes was...

"...I think I'm a little disappointed in Iska," Nene said.

"...He's let me down," Mismis agreed.

"...Imperial swordsman, I will be informing Lady Alice about this, so you should be prepared."

"There's been a huge misunderstanding!"

Beside him, Jhin artlessly tugged on Sisbell's hair and said in an exasperated tone, "Hey, keep it in your pants."

"Ow?! Wh-what do you think you're doing?! How could you be so rude as to tug on a girl's hair—?"

"We need to go after the person behind this."

"Ngh. I—I realize that...but do we really need to? I was so very afraid."

She turned around. Sisbell peered deeper into the mist as she scowled.

"Rin, over here."

"Lady Sisbell, do you know where that woman ran?" Rin asked.

"No. All she did was take me here. She told me she wanted to show me something and bound me in the wheelchair...but now that I'm getting a second look, this facility is monstrously big."

The princess gazed up at the furnaces that were releasing steam and light. Her lovely eyes were grim.

"It's releasing so much astral energy. There must be quite a large vortex underground here. Or perhaps several interconnected ones."

"But, Lady Sisbell, this is the Empire."

"The Empire also has vortices. Hey, Iska, do you remember what happened a year ago?"

"What?"

"I suppose I still haven't told you, then," Sisbell said. The princess's hair fluttered as she slowly turned around. She looked bitter as she spoke. "The reason why I rushed to the Empire from the Sovereignty in the first place when you saved me."

"...Oh."

Now that she'd pointed it out, this was the first time he'd realized it.

The witch breakout incident from one year prior. When he freed that imprisoned witch, he'd been convinced she was a prisoner of war from the battlefields.

...*But she couldn't have been.*

...*Sisbell is a princess, so she wouldn't have gone to the battlefield in the first place, considering what her astral power is.*

She wasn't like Alice, the Ice Calamity Witch.

Sisbell, who had lacked the ability to fight, wouldn't have gone to war.

"A year ago, I secretly attempted to sneak into the Empire without telling anyone. But then an Imperial soldier caught me, and I was arrested..."

She started walking again. A gigantic furnace appeared in the corner of her eye, towering over her.

"I wanted to look into the Empire's vortices. I was searching for furnaces exactly like these."

"Uh?! Wait, Lady Sisbell, what could you possibly mean by that?!"

"What I mean is—"

Crack.

The tip of her shoe had broken a pane of glass on the floor.

"What is this?"

Sisbell lifted her head. Something materialized out of the white mist in front of her, but it wasn't a furnace.

"......A water tank?"

The tank was made out of transparent panes of glass. Long and thin, it was large enough to hold a person. It almost looked like a test tube, though it was several hundred times larger than the ones used in scientific experiments.

"Rin, what do you think this is?"

"I am not sure myself. It seems that it shattered quite a while ago."

It had been broken from the inside, almost as though something had leaped out of it. The glass Sisbell had stepped on must have been a leftover shard.

"Rin, there's something written on the tank. Can you make it out?"

"............"

She strained to look where Sisbell was pointing.

"...It seems to say 'Subject E,' as far as I can tell."

"It's the subject Elletear's name."

They heard glass shatter. Someone had stepped across several shards.

"It seems you've found something very good, Princess Sisbell.

That was exactly the water tank I wanted to show you. It saves me the trouble of explaining."

A woman staggered in through the fog. Her red hair was a mess, as though it hadn't been combed in years. She looked thin and weak, almost sickly under the faded white coat that covered her shoulders.

...But what is this?

...I feel something ominous coming from her.

They had no idea who she was. Even Iska had subconsciously moved his hands to his astral swords.

"Kelvina!"

"Oh? It seems you've remembered my name, Princess Sisbell. Unfortunately, there's no value in knowing it. Not compared to the name of the witch who was in that tank."

The researcher scratched the back of her head and lifted her face. She looked up at the tank, which had been cracked in the center.

"Your sister was in there. First Princess Elletear Lou Nebulis IX."

"Stop talking!" yelled Third Princess Sisbell, baring her teeth. "...That joke again... What are you trying to say? That my own sister would volunteer to be held captive underground in the Empire? There's no way!"

"That subject came to the Empire of her own volition to become an experiment. It was two years ago."

"...Stop!"

"As a result, she was the first purebred the Empire had acquired. However, her astral power was laughably weak. She was the most pitiful witch I'd encountered, worthless for research purposes."

"I said shut your mouth!"

"Or so I thought at the time."

The red-haired researcher shrugged in resignation.

She forced a smile to her face.

"That was the greatest error of my life. I misjudged. Who would have known? Who indeed."

"...Wh-what are you saying?!"

"I've been telling you from the start, Princess Sisbell. This is the Birthplace of Witches. And it was here where I investigated the truth of this planet."

Her long red hair fluttered. The mad scientist Kelvina continued, practically singing her next statement. "She's on her way to becoming a true witch. A being that no one on this planet will be able to stop."

INTERMISSION

Greater Than the Joy of Man's Desires

"We have summoned the witch Elletear."

The Imperial assembly—the ultimate authoritative body of the Empire, which boasted the largest territory in the world, was casting a vote.

"Lift your face, Elletear. It has been two years since last you came to the Empire. How do you feel being back after so long?"

"So incredibly lucky."

Both her hands were restrained. The witch with the goddess-like face, Elletear, looked up with rapt attention.

Elletear Lou Nebulis IX.

Her fluttering hair was a gorgeous shade of emerald tinged with gold. Her beautiful face was so sweet and charming that it seemed fantastical. She could make a king surrender with just a single, furtive glance and a smile. If her absolute beauty could be called magic, no other person than her could more befittingly be dubbed a witch.

"It is nice to meet you all, Eight Great Apostles."

She was in the spacious parliamentary hall, standing on a platform in its center as she looked at each of the eight men and women in turn.

The Eight Great Apostles. These eight were the topmost people in the Imperial assembly, its leaders. Only the fuzzy outlines of their faces were visible on the monitors set up along the wall.

"You did well returning to us."

"Kelvina was incredibly disappointed when you left the facility so suddenly."

"Ha-ha. I am very sorry about that."

Her hands still bound in front of her, Elletear raised them to one cheek and smiled.

She sounded nostalgic as she spoke. "I was convinced I would be dealt with; Chief Kelvina would collect my astral body data and scratch her head day after day, after all. She claimed my compatibility ratio was too high."

"...Oh? So you remember?"

"...The reports stated you lost your sense of self during that time."

"I had bouts of lucidity. I was close to breaking, but somehow, I made *it* take a liking to me."

"...I see."

The Eight Great Apostles went silent.

Had any other members of the Imperial assembly witnessed the scene, they would undoubtedly be left speechless. It was impossible to measure just how curiously wary the Eight Great Apostles were of a single witch.

"So because of that," Elletear remarked, breaking the silence, "I escaped before I could be disposed of for being an out-of-control subject. But now that I think about it, I was mistaken. The Eight Great Apostles would never give such an order, of course."

"Yes, indeed."

"Anyone can make mistakes. We would never come to that determination after a proud princess such as yourself requested to become a subject of her own free will."

"Yes. I was quite rude to have assumed that."

She was so elegant, it was chilling. The princess of the Nebulis Sovereignty bowed.

"That is my account."

"Lift your head. You are no mere commoner."

"Though there is something we have to ask you."

"We only have your astral body data from two years ago. We believe that its consumption has progressed throughout your entire body since that time."

"Of course."

The emerald-haired witch placed her fingertips on her plump bosom.

"It makes me tremble in its own way. But increasingly...I feel comfortable integrating with it. The sensation of it making its way through my body is marvelous."

"_____"

"_____"

"I no longer fear anything."

Her fingers strained.

It was as though she was holding a large piece of fruit in a vise grip. From above her royal garments, she dug her fingers into her flesh, clutching her overflowing breasts.

"I feel as though I've finally reached the point where I shall soon be able to change the world."

Silence.

A deep, resounding quiet followed her statement, in which even the sound of the dust in the air seemed perceptible.

"Then we will ask you again."

"Elletear, what in the world is your aim?"

"..........." The witch slowly exhaled. "My aim? Why, I haven't changed in the slightest."

She removed her hands from her breast. As she gazed up at

these eight supreme authorities, her eyes looked as though they belonged to a different person from just seconds before. They were filled with lofty dignity.

"I want to reform the Sovereignty. Currently, only those who were born in the royal family are blessed, while weak astral mages are oppressed. I wish to mold it into a paradise without those qualities."

The Nebulis Sovereignty as it stood now was a false paradise. Only those born with powerful astral powers were revered. Since the moment they could perceive the world, the second and third princesses had been praised by the retainers. Kissing of the Zoa and Mizerhyby of the Hydra likely had been as well. They were purebreds, with astral powers befitting the next queen.

That is to say, no one else in the Sovereignty would ever see the limelight. The nation had remained unchanged since its founding; First Princess Elletear did not have a place in that system.

"My astral power is Voice. All it can do is mimic the tones of another. A parlor trick, an act fit for a bar. That's what they called it."

Elletear had been mortified. But she'd never shown anyone her tears, only letting herself cry in bed at night.

—*Even though I pushed my abilities to their utmost.*

—*And I worked harder than anyone in both my studies and etiquette so I would make a suitable queen.*

But no one had acknowledged that. Instead, she had been the target of continual ridicule, solely because her astral powers were weak.

"As you are aware, they said I was disqualified from being queen. Since childhood, many had jested that I would never attain the position."

"That is exactly right."

"The value of the astral power one possesses determines a person's worth. That is the Sovereignty."

"The Empire is not the nation most discriminatory against

witches. We remember you said that of the Nebulis Sovereignty two years ago."

That was why.

That was why the first princess had traveled to the Empire. She had offered her own body, the body of a purebred, to become a subject of the secret research that the Eight Great Apostles were conducting.

"Hence my desire to become a true witch."

"And what constitutes a true witch?"

"The ultimate, absolute, and singular witch—the last one in the world."

The witch princess looked up at the Eight Great Apostles. The princess who had lived as the weakest of the purebreds spoke of her dream.

"To the Sovereignty, I will have become a Calamity Witch. The queen will likely think me a foolish daughter, while my two sisters shall deride me as the sibling who lost her mind."

"And you are fine with that?"

"Yes."

"Even at the expense of your goddess-like beauty?"

"You could easily savor any man in the world with that body of yours. Do you not feel those human desires?"

"…Ah-ha."

The witch was maturer than she should have been in her twenty years. For the first time, she showed a mischievous smile that suited her age.

"Many erroneously believe that because of my body but despite my looks, I am but an innocent maiden at heart. Hedonism? Pleasure? I know nothing of the sort."

"And you have no interest in that?"

"I have already abandoned the joys of humanity."

"Magnificent."

Applause showered down on her from overhead. Unstinted

adoration resounded from the monitors above Elletear as she gazed upon them.

"What splendid resolve."

"In all likelihood, we shall work together once again. Our goals are the same."

"Yes, for what we seek is this planet's core."

Another shower of applause rained down on the witch's head.

"Now, Elletear, we welcome you to the Empire once again."

"We shall prepare a room for you. Please follow him."

Elletear turned around.

When had he appeared?

A redheaded knight had come to stand in the exit of the assembly hall. The Saint Disciple of the first seat, the "Flash" Knight, Joheim. She could not possibly forget him. She still had the faint traces of a wound from when his long sword had sliced through her chest. Then again, it likely would disappear in a few days.

"Will you be guiding me?"

"…………"

"Then I shall be counting on you."

The Saint Disciple of the first seat turned.

Come with me. Though he did not say that aloud, Elletear began to follow again. She turned her back to the Eight Great Apostles.

"First, my birthplace. And after, I can change the Empire," the witch murmured through voluptuous lips.

CHAPTER 6

Cherub

1

Imperial territory. Easternmost Altoria jurisdiction.

A remote location far to the east of the Imperial capital. An underground facility.

"You're blessed. You've seen Elletear, two years later, right?"

A smashed water tank. The researcher who looked up at a tag engraved with the words SUBJECT E did not attempt to hide the glee in her voice.

"Vichyssoise served as a good example. A subject who has finished fusing with the astral power will, without exception, show signs of deviating from human physiology, after all. How about Elletear?"

She glanced at Sisbell, then Rin, then the members of Unit 907 as she spoke quickly.

"Did she still look human on the outside? What color was her skin? Her eyes? Did she sprout fangs? Oh, or perhaps two heads—?"

A gunshot.

It pierced through the mist filling the vast hall and grazed Kelvina's cheek.

A welling of blood...

Red slowly oozed out of her wounded cheek.

"Who asked for the talk show?"

The silver-haired sniper pointed the muzzle of his gun at her. They were about ten yards away. Jhin could probably snipe Kelvina accurately to a single hair on her head.

"We're real members of the Imperial forces. We're inquiring on suspicions you've broken Imperial law."

"Yes, I suppose you *are* Imperial soldiers." The researcher looked at them with apparent surprise. "I would have expected the Sovereignty's assassins to come to retrieve Sisbell."

"Yeah, I don't know about them... I know about that witch Vichyssoise, though. Are you the one who made her the way she is?"

"She was such a lovely subject. Her resonance ratio with *it* wasn't too high or too low."

"What is 'it'?"

"This planet's nightmare."

"Huh?"

"The thing that the Astrals revered, which they dubbed the Great Planetary Calamity. Similar to astral power, yet different. If I had to make a comparison, I'd liken it to a single poisonous moth among ten billion butterflies. Mistake that moth for a lovely butterfly, and you'll end up all the worse for it."

"............"

"Very rarely, it will rise from the planet's core through a vortex. When it manifests, we call it the Great Contact, and we abstract the energy in order to bring it here to—"

"That's enough. You're wasting time." Jhin cut her off. He took a look around the gigantic furnaces lining the large hall and then the broken tank. "Basically, this was human experimentation. That's what you were up to."

"Conducting tests on astral bodies."

"I don't care how you misconstrue it. Boss, Nene."

As the two of them readied their high-voltage stun guns, Jhin motioned at a furnace behind him with his chin.

"Take pictures for proof while we still can. We need that, and witnesses. She's got to have people captured here to use as experimental subjects. Find them and free them."

"You won't find any." Kelvina didn't even wipe the blood from her cheek as she shook her head. "I want subjects who are purebred. Very difficult to find in the Empire, I'm afraid. That was why the Hydra's offer was so valuable and why I was dancing for joy when Elletear offered herself. And also why…" She turned, then pointed a finger, rough from exposure to chemicals, at the princess with the strawberry-blond hair. "I won't let you escape."

"Eep?!"

Kelvina's maddened eyes glistened as they locked onto Sisbell. When she felt that stare pierce into her, Sisbell unconsciously took a step back.

"Your body is invaluable. It will be a delight to—"

A gunshot. When the second one rang through the hall, the researcher staggered.

It had hit her left cheek. This time, Jhin's bullet dug a fraction of an inch deeper into Kelvina.

"Only answer the question."

"…………"

Drip. The mad scientist kept silent as she stared at the blood that blotted the ground.

"…"

"We're not going along with your screwed-up fantasies, so let us take you in nice and quietly. We'll tell HQ and hand you over to the closest base."

"Now, that will be an issue." The mad scientist was still staring at the ground. "The things we're developing here are delicate, you see. Someone needs to watch over the apparatus values, and the place needs to be kept at a specific temperature and chemical concentration at all times. If I'm not around, everything will be for nothing."

"Sounds just peachy to me." Jhin was serious. "We arrest you and destroy this creepy facility. Seems like two birds with one stone to me."

"...I should be the one saying that."

Since when had she brought *that* out? Kelvina held a small device that fit perfectly in her hand. It was a remote control with just a single button.

"An Imperial unit will be an excellent use for this experiment. You came at exactly the right time."

"Hey, you better not move—"

"You're too late."

Jhin hadn't even had time to shoot. The moment the mad scientist's finger touched the button, groans issued from the furnaces in the hall.

Klunk.

Like fireworks, the glass lids on the furnaces burst away.

Steam bellowed out of them. Then astral energy erupted from their containers, lighting the hall as though they were in broad daylight.

"What is this?! What's with this light...?!"

They covered their eyes with their hands, but it was still too bright. The astral glow was so strangely powerful that they couldn't stare directly at it. Faced with that, Iska felt a cold shiver travel down his spine.

"It couldn't be......"

He had seen this before.

He was sure he had seen this astral energy before. And he

hadn't been the only one. In the independent state of Alsamira, Nene and Sisbell had also witnessed it alongside him.

"Iska. There has definitely got to be something in the machinery in there!"
"Object! What are you hiding inside you?!"

It was the same light that had come streaming out of the witch-hunting machine that had gone after Sisbell, the Object. Back then, the thing that had been hiding in the mechanized soldier must have been...

"Arise, Beasts of Katalisk."

At Kelvina's order, the furnaces burst to pieces. Indistinct bodies of light leaped from them. They had humanoid silhouettes and glittered violet; light similar to astral energy poured out of them.

"...It's the same as back then!" When Sisbell beheld the things resembling astral power overhead, her voice cracked. "Iska, it's the monster that was in the Object!"

"...It looks that way to me, too."

Iska readied his black astral sword and sucked in a breath.

He never would have thought this would happen. Not in his wildest dreams would he have thought he'd discover the mystery of that unidentified mechanical soldier in a place like this.

"So you were the one who made these things, Kelvina?!"

"Oh, so you know of them?"

The redheaded mad scientist lifted an eyebrow.

"Their name for the time being is Beasts of Katalisk. As you can see, they are artificial astral powers. They'll serve as next-gen energy for the Imperial forces' weapons. Though I just call them my pets."

"...Pets?"

"Yes, come to think of it, I do remember the Eight Great Apostles provisioning me with an Object into which to load one of them. If you witnessed it, you were given a very valuable experience."

...Seeing her pet, she says?

...That thing isn't cute or *cuddly!*

One of the Beasts of Katalisk had attacked Sisbell and nearly destroyed an entire country in the process. He couldn't help but feel a chill, realizing that these things had been mass-produced.

"I get it now."

He heard someone kick forward off the floor. Rin held a dagger as she headed straight for Kelvina without so much as glancing at the pet above her.

"Taking care of you first will be quickest."

"Disperse."

"Rin, get down!"

Iska grabbed her arm from behind and forced her to the ground.

It had been an order to self-destruct.

There was a flare.

The pet above them swelled and immediately burst into a ball of violet flame.

"...Why, you!"

Rin looked indignant as she rose to her feet. Kelvina had already disappeared.

She had slipped into the mist. Her fluttering coat disappeared farther into the hall.

"Sisbell, we need to get outside now while we still can! The other artificial astral powers might start going on the move."

The embers from the explosion flitted as Iska turned around. He faced the woman standing there dumbstruck.

"Commander, you know how to get out of here. Take Nene and Jhin, too. Once you escape, send a message to the closest Imperial unit you can!"

"W-wait, Iska! What about you?!"

"I can't just leave that woman be."

"But...!"

"Let's go." Jhin grabbed Sisbell's shoulder.

He stared at the steam still coming from the furnaces. "There's no point to this if you don't make it out alive. Why do you think we came all the way here?"

"......Ugh."

The princess bit her lip.

Then she immediately started running, her strawberry-blond hair undulating as she went.

"Iska, you're not allowed to die until you become my guard! Jhin, please do all in your power to take me to the exit!"

She raced into the fog. Iska wasn't even able to watch her go. He turned in the opposite direction. The way Kelvina had escaped.

He started to sprint. Beside him ran a certain brunette.

"Rin?"

"If I leave you on your own, Lady Sisbell will scold me later."

The furnaces groaned and shuddered. As they passed them, Alice's attendant added, "Also..."

"I don't want to admit this, but it is clear the first princess is connected to the Empire. Just like the Hydra, she is a traitor to our country."

"............"

"I must report this to the queen. And to Lady Alice as well, of course."

There were at least two conspiring with the Empire.

They had more or less speculated as much was the case since they had been in the Sovereignty.

"*There were* two *people behind the coup. That was Elletear and you*—the one who invited the Imperial forces here."

Jhin had been the one to see it.

The Hydra's head of house, Talisman, had all but confirmed it at the Lou's villa.

...*How awful for Rin and Alice.*

...That someone from their own family was responsible for the assassination attempt on the queen.

It was of no relevance to Imperial soldiers. Try as he might to remind himself of that, he still imagined Alice in a deplorable state. At the same time, he also shuddered.

"Former Saint Disciple Iska. Won't you become my subordinate?"

"I want to crush present-day Nebulis into smithereens. I want to overturn it from its roots."

· She had told him everything. It had been so illogical that he had convinced himself it had to be a joke.

...It happened at the Lou's villa.

...We were alone together, but would any normal person really be able to declare that so openly?

He couldn't see the point of this. What was it that First Princess Elletear wanted? What could be so worthwhile that she'd join the Empire and offer up her body to undergo a ghastly process to become a witch?

"There she is!"

Iska turned when Rin said that. Passing through a corridor the hall led into, they ran deeper in after the redheaded researcher. As she went through the mechanized doors, they closed.

"She's planning on locking herself in?! Wrench it open!"

The earth doll leaped out, wedging its fingers into the entrance as it slid shut before prying the door open by force. Iska and Rin both leaped through the opening.

There was another large hall. Ahead of them, they saw a furnace that was larger than the others. It was likely two times bigger than the dozen or so machines in the other hall. Turbulent, roaring astral light was emitting from it.

And farther away from that furnace...

"We've cornered you."

Rin was closing in on Kelvina, whose back was facing them.

"You're not doing astral power research. What you are carrying out is blasphemy to the astral powers."

"..."

"I wish I could take you into the Sovereignty, but at the very least, I will have you pay for the crimes you committed against Lady Elletear."

"____"

"Do you know of a bird called the crossbill—an iska in our tongue?"

The mad scientist turned around.

Her white coat still clung to her as she did so.

"It's a tiny bird. No one would give it a passing thought if it flew by them. But that bird has a very unusual feature—its upper and lower beaks don't match. Because of that, there are many folktales about the iska and its mismatched beak. That it pulled out a lance that had gored a sage or that it stopped the arrow of a demon."

Kelvina's eyes.

They were trained on Iska.

"Your astral swords are very similar, former Saint Disciple Iska. Black and white. Even their lengths are different. They don't match at all. They're just like an iska's beak."

"...What are you trying to say?"

"There's a secret story to them. Those astral swords."

B-bmp.

Was that the sound of a gigantic monster's heartbeat? For a moment, Iska nearly believed that as the hall quivered strangely from a palpitation.

That sound had come from Kelvina's chest.

B-bmp, b-bmp..., it went.

"I am an Imperial. I'll have you know I wasn't born with astral power. It takes time to force someone to become a witch. Based on my third attempt, it takes six minutes and twenty-nine seconds to reach stability."

A howl echoed throughout the area. Violet flames erupted from the mad scientist and engulfed her whole body.

"Wha—?!" Rin's eyes opened wide. "Iska, this is the same as Vichyssoise..."

"Get back, Rin!"

The two both leaped away at the same time. A purple blaze swelled from the floor where they had been standing and engulfed it.

"Ah, I see. So you've already fought Vichyssoise, then."

Beyond the flames, what was once the astral researcher Kelvina Sofita Elmos began to transform.

The wicked star mutant, Katalisk's Angel.

The clothes she had been wearing blew away. Her red hair stiffened before their eyes, and her body turned half transparent, like clouded glass.

...She's the same as Vichyssoise.

...No. If she is, then what are those thorns on her back?

As Kelvina transformed, black things started to protrude from her spine. The thin, needlelike protrusions grew steadily until they formed what looked like distorted wings.

"Not a witch but a malevolent angel..."

The former human being spread her wings.

"I progressed with my research using the same surgery performed on Vichyssoise. After changing the concentration of the agent, this was the result. Though the cost of rejection is greater."

It was as if she was ogling them. Malevolent angel Kelvina looked down on the pair who had followed her from the hall.

"The era of astral power will soon end. With the dawn of a new power."

2

An unnamed laboratory.

In the basement of the building that she knew only as the Birthplace of Witches, she continued to sprint breathlessly forward.

"Miss Sisbell, over here!"

"Y-yes, I see!"

In response to Nene waving for her to come, Sisbell ran up the stairs leading to the ground level.

"Miss Sisbell, is there a hidden door somewhere?! Like an emergency exit to get outside?!"

"…I don't remember. But since they kept me underground, I think there must be a direct way out of here."

The pharmacy.

Sisbell bit her lip as she glanced around the unfamiliar room.

She had been unconscious. She didn't know where she was. Even now, running after Nene and Commander Mismis, she felt as though she was wandering through a maze.

"Guess all we can do is go back the way we came. I don't feel too comfortable running through that dark floor again, though."

"Jhin, um…it hasn't been long since we met each other, all things considered, but…" Sisbell turned only her head to the sniper, who brought up the rear. "Thank you. You shot her for me, didn't you?"

"Why are you thanking me?"

"…Never mind. I'm sure you understand, so I won't mention it again."

It was the timing of his shot.

She couldn't believe it wasn't intentional on his part.

"How about Elletear?"

"Did she still look human on the outside? What color was her skin? Her eyes? Did she sprout fangs? Oh, or perhaps two heads—?"

* * *

Kelvina had treated her sister like a monster.

At the time, Sisbell must have looked horribly enraged, but Jhin's bullet had silenced Kelvina.

"I feel relieved. But it would have been even better if she hadn't gotten away with just a grazed cheek. If only she had been punched right in the face."

"That's Iska's job. Not mine. Also, keep running."

"Y-yes, I know!"

She was following Nene and Commander Mismis as quickly as she could. There was no light coming from the ceiling. Before her eyes, the pair disappeared into the darkness.

"Wh-where are you, Commander Mismis?! Miss Nene!"

"Miss Sisbell, over here!" Nene's voice echoed against the walls. It was all Sisbell could go on in this pitch-black maze. The floor was already dark as it was, and if there were any obstacles, she was liable to trip. "Ugh, enough... I have no choice."

Sisbell put her hand to her collar. She unbuttoned it, exposing her chest—her astral crest. There was a faint glow. The match-like light was much better than total darkness.

"...Even I am aware that my astral light is hardly useful."

"Seems handy to me."

"It makes me feel like a human electric generator, so I'm not fond of it. Also, Jhin, please refrain from staring. It would not be gentlemanly of you to peek at a girl's chest."

"Is there even anything to look at?"

"There is... Mghf?!"

"Shush." Jhin had latched onto her from behind. He had placed a hand over her mouth.

Maybe she shouldn't have shouted? That was what crossed her mind, at least. Jhin, on the other hand, was frozen in place, staring at the pharmacy.

"...That light."

They caught glimpses of an intense violet luminescence. Just as Sisbell noticed it, the door of the pharmacy flew open and crumpled from an explosion. Out from the flames crawled something humanoid and spectral. It was one of the artificial astral powers—a monster.

"Could it have been following me...?!"

"Run!"

She didn't need him to tell her. Before Jhin could yell, Sisbell had already started taking off as fast as she could down the dark corridor.

"I have no interest in humans. But you are special, former Saint Disciple Iska."

The hall was filled with faint astral light.

The once-human thing, now half transparent like glass, slowly rose. It was like a vile angel, free from the shackles of gravity.

"I wanted to have a superhuman like a Saint Disciple as one of my subjects. I begged the Eight Great Apostles for one. And as luck would have it, it seems I'll be able to get one myself."

The Eight Great Apostles. Iska scowled internally when he heard those words. At that moment, two sensations overcame him. He was simultaneously shocked at the perpetrators, yet certain it had been them. The two opposing feelings clashed and swirled in his chest.

...This unsettling research. I knew that someone big had to be behind it.

...But the Eight Great Apostles of all people!

Even the Imperial headquarters was probably unaware. They had come into contact with the most dangerous darkness lurking in the Empire.

"That is why—"

"You sure run your mouth in combat." He heard someone leap from the ground. The malevolent angel Kelvina hadn't even noticed. Rin, who had been standing next to Iska, had swerved around behind the woman.

"I'll pluck those grotesque wings."

She moved like a leopard, pouncing from the floor nearly three yards into the air before she brought down the two large daggers she held.

Klink.

A dull sound.

Followed by the shattering of two daggers echoing throughout the place.

"But these were precious blades from the royal family!"

"I'm just about as hard as the Planetary Stronghold. Even a shot from a tank wouldn't break me."

Kelvina's wings wriggled. They weren't composed of plumes but rather a countless number of protuberances from her body. Each of them had begun to glow. They were like a giant machine gun barrel on the verge of firing.

The luminescence started to converge. Dozens of lights gathered into one and brightened the hall as though it was midday.

"Rin, don't let that glow hit you!"

"Nightgaze."

The malevolent angel released it from her wings—the same blast of ultimate astral energy that the Object had once shot. The belt of light let out a shrill sound as it scorched the air, rocketing toward Rin.

"Rin!"

"Kick me away!"

Rin, who was stuck in midair, was kicked by the earth soldier that had leaped up with the luminescence… It touched the beam and evaporated.

"You blasted away my doll?!"

Rin turned pale as the light that had barely grazed her began to melt through the floor. It even touched the back wall and created a large explosion.

"Guh?!" Rin landed as the wind from the blast hit her.

"I have no interest in you, witch."

Dozens of lights burned in the other wing. They once again converged and lit the hall with rays as strong as the sun.

"You think I would let you?"

The flash cut off halfway. Iska had brought down his black sword after leaping in front of Rin.

"You severed the light?"

"I saw this shot from the Object. I remember it, whether I like it or not."

Cold sweat rolled down his back. He tried his best to keep her from realizing his right arm was paralyzed as he gave the malevolent angel the most natural glare he could muster.

…What I did just now was reckless.

…Cutting through that beam was nothing short of a miracle. And it's not like I knew I'd be successful.

In this instance, Iska couldn't rely on his skills. But if he hadn't taken a risk, Rin would have been scorched out of existence.

"I suppose I should have expected this, but you were wrong to save the witch." The malevolent angel Kelvina jeered. **"You cannot move that right arm of yours. I'm sure the pain of holding that sword is excruciating."**

"……Tsk."

"My astral energy is adhering to your right arm. When you sliced through the glow, it grazed your right hand slightly, yes?"

Blood dripped from Iska's right hand. As though she was taking her time to observe it, the malevolent angel's eyes narrowed.

"Still, your astral swords are truly magnificent. If you can cut through my astral energy, there is a possibility they could even be used on the planet's demise."

"......What are you talking about?"

"I have a great spirit of inquiry."

The malevolent angel stretched her arms into the air. It was as though she were compelling him to offer up the blade.

"My thirst for that sword is rising. I hear it is the ultimate instrument, forged by the Astrals themselves."

"Shut up, monster."

"Hmm?"

That had come from a corner of the vast hall. The girl, who had been thrown aside by the astral energy, rose to her feet. Rin ran straight at the malevolent angel Kelvina, still in midair. Even from Iska's perspective, her charge was absurd.

"You can't! Don't go near her, Rin!"

It was too sloppy.

She had just broken her dagger without making a scratch on the malevolent angel. Most importantly, she couldn't use her astral power. There wasn't any earth for her to control.

"You're desperate, then." Kelvina sounded disappointed. **"How pitiable for an earth witch. Take away soil to manipulate, and you're powerless. I'm sure that soldier was your final pawn."**

"..."

"What do you think you will accomplish with your fist—? Ughhhhhh?!"

The malevolent angel Kelvina staggered. A human girl much smaller than her had jabbed her in midair and sent her flying. She wouldn't have seen that coming.

Since Kelvina was a mass of astral energy, no one in their right mind would have thought a mere human fist would work on her. That should have been the case, yet she had been clobbered anyway.

"You were saying?"

Rin turned after landing.

As though showing off her right fist, she lifted it toward the monster in the air. It was covered in earth.

"Astral energy works against you. That makes things easy. I formed a sphere of soil around my fist using astral power and nailed you as hard as I could."

"............"

A small crack had formed in the angel's cheek. It didn't look particularly painful, but the blow was enough to show the threat that Rin posed as an astral mage.

"Earth witch. Was that your astral power?"

"Isn't that obvious?"

"...But you had no earth to use."

"It's right here."

Crack.

Below Rin's feet, a flask filled with soil broke.

"Earth astral mages are powerless without our element? We've known that since a hundred years ago. For generations and generations before me."

The Imperial mad scientist had underestimated her. She had underestimated the wisdom and tenacity of astral mages who had waged a war over a hundred years.

"Obviously, I wouldn't come here empty-handed."

She pulled up her skirt.

As she did so, boldly exposing her pale thighs, she revealed dozens of glass bottles filled with soil lining the underside of her outfit.

Those made an almost beautiful array of sounds as they crashed and broke at Rin's feet one after another. It captivated the malevolent angel. It was elegant—a type of art, almost a sleight of hand.

"One jar holds about fifty grams. It's only a little over two pounds of soil from twenty bottles."

The dirt rose.

When it came into contact with the earth astral mage Rin Vispose's astral energy, it took form in the palm of her hand, transforming into earth daggers.

"Perfect for tearing off your wings."

"...How adorable."

Kelvina watched as though enraptured. The inhuman monster stared down at the girl below her.

"I didn't think much of you, but it seems you are a diamond in the rough, witch. If you are an assassin who came to save the princess, then might you be one of the Astral Guards who exclusively protect the royal family?"

"I don't feel like responding."

"I have all the time in the world to look into it. That is no obstacle."

Rin's eyes were emotionless, like the sand of a desert. The girl, who didn't hide her animosity, lifted her lips into a smile as she looked at the inhuman angel with more and more mirth.

"Another quality witch in addition to Princess Sisbell."

"I told you."

Rin's footsteps echoed loudly in the hall as she leaped from the ground. It was nearly explosive.

"A blade made from the earth."

"Come, astral flames."

The witch's and malevolent angel's voices overlapped. The air burst with a roar. Purple flames that were hot as the sun surged from all over Kelvina's body. Rin didn't stop as she closed the distance between them as quickly as she could.

"Violet Asteroid Belt."

The blaze swirled, swelling into a fireball that could engulf Rin.

"Tsk." Rin clicked her tongue at the inferno before her. The next instant, the girl picked up speed. Tearing off the excess fabric of her skirt, which was long enough to reach the ground, she turned it into a miniskirt that exposed her thighs.

"Is that your combat outfit?"

"You think I'm wearing this because it's my taste?"

She leaned down, skimming the ground to slip past the flames, and came up right before Kelvina's eyes. Rin aimed for the center of her chest and thrust her dagger. Even Iska barely realized it.

The angel had disappeared.

Without any warning.

Rin's blade gouged the air. The monster wasn't there anymore.

"This is the reason…"

"…Impossible?!"

"The reason I called myself an angel."

The malevolent angel was above Rin's head.

How had she moved there?

Even Iska, who had been watching from afar, shuddered after seeing everything from start to finish. It wasn't that he hadn't just not seen her move. He hadn't been able to *perceive* it.

…There wasn't any sound or indication. Not even a breeze.

…She appeared as suddenly as she disappeared. Does she teleport like you can with astral power?!

But this was different from teleportation astral power.

That movement couldn't be produced by an astral mage. It was a phenomenon of astral power—one that transcended the laws of physics.

She was of a higher order than humanity could ever attain. Now it was dawning on Iska why Kelvina had called herself an angel—a being of divine allegory.

"Just one to start."

"Guh?!"

She brought her distorted wings down on Rin's head.

They fell like a guillotine. Rin's daggers returned to earth in an instant and reassembled into a shield.

She blocked the wings.

"Very quick at reconstructing, I see. Now you're getting interesting," the malevolent angel said almost affectionately. With a wing, she lightly pushed down on the shield Rin held. **"You can**

still be good for research even if your bones and flesh are slightly squashed. So don't worry about me crushing you."

"...You monster..." Rin gritted her teeth as she kept the shield up. Though she was pushing back with all she had, it wouldn't budge, almost as though she were pushing back against a steel wall.

"You fiend... How far must you stray from humanity before you're satisfied?!"

"Ah, praise."

"...I see. In that case, I'll think of you as human. No more holding back."

The earth shield burst. The soil, which had turned into a whip in Rin's hands, coiled around Kelvina's wing.

"You can't move if I catch you."

"What?"

"Get her, Iska!" Rin howled. Even before she screamed, however, Iska had already taken a straight shot at the malevolent angel. He could cut her with the astral sword. They had proof it could from the battle with Vichyssoise.

"Tsk." For the first time, Kelvina showed signs of dismay. Though her wings were still caught in the bonds of earth, she turned around and thrust her hand in Iska's direction.

"Though I'm loath to lose a precious sample...turn to ash."

The raging astral flames shot out.

The fireball split into an innumerable number of embers and rose into the air, then showered down on Iska like a sudden rain.

"Your right arm— What?!"

He cut off Kelvina's wail and simply kept heading forward. Iska gauged the trajectory of the fireball that tinged the entire hall violet as he brought up his astral sword.

"Hah!"

He cut through the astral inferno raining down ahead of him, then severed the fireball that came at him next. Then Iska dodged the flames coming at him from an angle above and sliced the flames following him along the ground behind him with near-perfect precision.

He did all of that with the black astral sword in his left hand.

...I knew it.

...You haven't changed on the inside at all, Kelvina!

Though she had transformed into something that transcended him, at her core, she still thought and acted like a researcher.

All the Saint Disciples could use either hand as though it were their dominant. Through training, he had developed these skills that no ordinary person could imagine.

It was the final step.

The last step before his sword was within striking distance of Kelvina.

"Beautiful."

Her smile was inhuman.

"Saint Disciples truly are magnificent. Your technique in battle is like a god of war's. Though you rely on intuition, you certainly have the judgment to know how to ensure your survival. You truly are a superhuman soldier."

"...What are you...?"

"But you are nothing compared to an angel."

Her entire body glittered. It was different from when she had been overflowing with astral flames. Her jewellike, transparent form glistened like a pearl—then exploded.

It burst into thousands of tiny particles of light and melted away into the air.

...She exploded?!

...She self-destructed?! No, it's too weak for that.

He would expect a giant blast as powerful as that to pulverize the entire hall. An overwhelming sense of dread ran through him.

...Which manifested as a scream from Rin.

"Iska, behind you!"

What?

He hadn't had time to even wonder that. Rin's eyes opened wide as she shouted. At that moment, one thing was clearer than all else—he could sense the threat of death approaching him from above.

A flash.

As Iska threw himself away, he felt a great amount of astral energy graze his neck.

A fraction of a second.

Had he hesitated to leap, his head would have been sliced clean off his neck.

"Top marks for your quick thinking, earth witch."

Iska turned. Up above, he saw untold thousands of pearls of lights coalescing together. They morphed into an angel, flapping her malformed wings.

"You thought you could use your earth astral power to keep ahold of me so I wouldn't be able to use my Leap? That's spot-on. Since there's astral energy in the soil you control, it's the one snare that could possibly capture my physical form."

Kelvina had perfectly reshaped. After turning into particles of light and fully disappearing, she had re-formed behind Iska. But until Rin had yelled, he hadn't sensed her in the slightest.

…I knew it.

…Her teleportation doesn't have any tells and can be performed instantaneously. It's beyond the five human senses!

This was a first.

The first time anyone had so easily taken him by surprise from behind.

"Unfortunate, isn't it, witch? The deficiencies of that soil you manipulate. The astral energy you could put into just a thousand grams of dirt wasn't enough to bind me."

"…Huh!" Rin scowled.

At that moment, Iska and Rin realized what truly separated this monster from the rest.

This wasn't the same as facing a human.

And she wasn't a machine like the Object.

They were fighting astral power itself. That was what this was.

"What a lovely face you're making, witch. And you as well, former Saint Disciple Iska. It seems to have dawned on you. Human abilities will never match that of an angel. This isn't a matter of being on different levels. There's a disparity in our potential."

Malevolent angel Kelvina flung open her arms. Ominous astral light overflowed from the great number of protuberances that made up her wings.

...And then she disappeared.

Without sound or trace.

"Damn it. Where is she coming from next...?"

"I'm behind you, witch."

The sound was dull.

Iska hadn't even had the time to yell. The girl flew into the air like a piece of paper as Kelvina's wings blew her away.

"Rin!"

"......Ugh..."

Her back crashed into the concrete floor. Her whole body convulsed as she tried to scream, but nothing came out.

"Rin!"

Iska stepped forward suddenly.

He had changed direction.

He ran straight for the monster that had blown away Rin.

"You're abandoning her, then? How fitting for an Imperial— abandoning a witch—"

"Nine seconds."

"Huh?!"

"That's the amount of time between that thing you called a Leap. Am I wrong?"

She could invoke her imperceptible teleportation for nine

seconds. Once she did, it was unlikely anyone could perceive her approach.

...The next time she uses it, even I won't be able to dodge her.

...This is my only chance!

He didn't have the time to rush to Rin. He needed to end this in the nine seconds he had.

"But you only have five seconds left."

She sneered—the sneer of something that had given up its humanity.

"You think you can capture me?"

"Not me."

He stepped forward without hesitation. Gripping the astral sword in his left hand, Iska headed toward the malevolent angel that was rising close to the ceiling.

"But Rin."

Krish.

A fissure opened in the wall directly to Kelvina's side.

An earth golem leaped in, smashing the wall.

It attacked.

It pinned the airborne angel's arms behind her back. It took only a second for the whole thing to be done.

"A golem?!"

Kelvina hadn't expected any of this.

The witch was unconscious. The golem shouldn't have been able to move without her orders. And besides, since when had something so large as a golem—?

"From the start," Iska said.

He gripped the sword in his left hand. Iska leaped at the monster.

"That golem was waiting outside the building this whole time."

"Huh?!"

"As long as she's got earth, she can do anything. As soon as this battle started, Rin instructed the golem to come underground."

Then she had made it stand by behind the wall. It had waited for the moment the malevolent angel Kelvina had come close enough that it could break through the wall to take her by surprise.

...The time interval is nine seconds.

...We weren't defeating her in that time. All we needed to do was catch her.

In the golem's net.

All he'd needed to do was force her into the trap.

"Impossible."

The mad scientist's eyes went wide. She had finally realized it. In order to make sure she had the nine seconds before she could use her invincible Leap, she had jumped away from Iska as he closed in.

And that was checkmate.

In fleeing from Iska, she had fallen into the trap of the golem waiting behind the wall.

Nine seconds had passed.

The malevolent angel couldn't use her teleportation—her trump card.

The vast astral energy of the earth golem holding on to her prevented her from invoking her power.

"I have a piece of advice. From one Imperial to another."

"...Impossible."

"Don't underestimate an astral mage's tenacity. That's the first thing they teach you in the Imperial forces."

A flash of the black blade.

With his left hand, Iska brought down his sword and sliced through Kelvina's wings.

"...Ah!"

They fell.

Kelvina had lost control now that her wings were gone. As the golem still kept her entire body restrained...

*　　*　　*

...she crashed through the glass lid to the furnace and plummeted into it.

Roar!

Astral energy surged out of the furnace.

Not just from one of them. The furnace next to the one Kelvina had tumbled into also ferociously erupted, like a volcano, and started to emit an intense light.

"...It's resonating...?!"

Rin lifted her face as the place trembled.

"...The astral powers trapped in there are trying...to escape..."

It wasn't just human beings.

There were also astral powers being held against their will in the forbidden lab—and they had been released.

———————

Elza's Sarcophagus. Birthplace of Witches.

First aboveground level. Eastern facade.

Unit 907's voices echoed across the lightless floor where all windows had been sealed.

"Miss Sisbell, quickly!"

"Jhin Big Bro, what about your gun?!"

"No use. Can't hurt these guys with firearms. The bullets just go straight through them... Just run!"

She had no idea where they were heading. Sisbell relied on Nene's and Commander Mismis's voices ahead of them as Jhin's bellows pushed her forward from behind. She continued sprinting as fast as she could.

"Jhin! Can't you do something about this...?"

"I just tried. How am I supposed to shoot a monster when the bullets go right through it? Best way out of this is to run."

"...Wait, that sound."

Skreeeeee.

The screech was like glass being scraped. Sisbell turned around and found the concrete wall right in front of her was glittering violet and melting like sludge.

"I-it's behind the wall?! Did they get ahead of us?!"

"Get down!"

"...Ah!"

The silver-haired young man pushed her down.

Sisbell tumbled to the floor and watched as the concrete wall burst open from a terrific explosion as easily as someone slicing through paper. A dense cloud of dust rose from the wall. She saw the faint outline of humanoid astral energy appear from behind the smoke. It was radiant and eerie, like a ghost.

"...Artificial astral power!"

It was one of the monsters who emitted astral power–like light. It must have been set loose from the research room underground and followed them all the way here. Since guns were useless against it, all they could do was run from it now.

"Over here! Over here, Miss Sisbell, Jhin!" Commander Mismis beckoned for them to come from farther into the hallway.

How far had they run already? Her side was throbbing from sprinting at full force, which she rarely did, but she would have to keep it up if she wanted to live.

...There's still no sign of Iska and Rin even though they're supposed to meet us here.

...How is their battle against that mad scientist going?

She hid herself in the shadows of the hall.

"Haah...tsk...ah..."

"Miss Sisbell, are you all right?"

"Y-yes..."

Her chest throbbed so much, it felt like it would burst. Even just responding to Nene took all she had.

153

...But we did gain something from this.

...We finally know what the witch Vichyssoise is and what was in the core of the Object.

Someone had been conducting forbidden research.

The monsters coming to attack her. Now that she knew they were the product of Imperial experiments, she had to find some way to tell the queen.

On the other hand, there was a new mystery.

She needed to find out what "that" thing the mad scientist had kept going on about was.

"The thing that the Astrals revered, which they dubbed the Great Planetary Calamity. Similar to astral power, yet different..."

"Very rarely, it will rise from the planet's core through a vortex."

Astrals? The Great Planetary Calamity?

What were those things? Even Sisbell, who had listened in on conversations within the Nebulis Sovereignty using her Illumination astral power, had never heard those words before.

"......Found you."

That had come from directly below her.

The moment Sisbell heard the murmur that sounded almost like a repulsive curse, her whole body shuddered.

She felt something brush her ankle.

The instant she realized it, something gripped her ankle with unfathomable force. A faintly glowing humanoid shape that looked almost like a ghost was peeking out from the dusty floor. Only its head was aboveground.

...But?!

...Did it rise directly from the underground lab through the floor all the way up here?!

She had been caught.

The moment she realized that, it was all too late.

"Miss Sisbell?!"

"Damn it! Let her go!"

Jhin's bullets and Nene's stun gun wouldn't work against it. The artificial astral power, whose head and arm were the only things visible above the concrete floor, began to glow steadily brighter as it kept a hold over her ankle.

"Life-form integra."

"Huh?!"

Sisbell recalled the crimson disaster she had seen in the independent state.

A flash of ultimate luminescence that had scorched away everything. If something like that was unleashed here, even if they weren't directly hit, the heat wave would blast away every human being in the area without a trace.

"...That's enough! You can all leave me behind!" she yelled.

Even she hadn't understood why she had yelled that now, at the last minute.

The Imperials were supposed to be enemies. Their lives weren't even worth chewing gum wrappers to her. The most they amounted to was valuable hostages. A Nebulis Sovereignty princess such as herself had been taught that for many long years. She still believed that now. The former Saint Disciple who had value as a guard was the only one who was special.

She didn't care about the other three in the unit...or so she had thought.

"You've done enough! So you don't have to...!"

The ominous light gathered.

It released destructive luminescence that would turn everything into dust.

Sew sia lukia Sec amuy. Sera lu E lukia Ses qelno—I will show you my memories, so you show me the future.

*   *   *

The astral energy burst from the underground furnaces.

Dozens, no, hundreds of faint glittering lights blasted away the life-form integra that had just been fired. The glow from the astral powers washed away the artificial astral power itself.

"............Huh?"

Sisbell couldn't even imagine what had happened. She had no way of knowing that right at that moment, in the underground hall, Iska and Rin had destroyed the furnaces.

"...I'm...saved...?"

Sisbell looked up, taken aback. The astral light that pierced through the roof and surged out left a glittering rainbow behind as it disappeared far into the blue sky.

3

Fire, light, and a rumble that shook the depths of the earth.

It was almost like the inside of a vortex. The expansive astral energy swirled, seeming almost divine as it did so in the underground hall. It was enveloped by a brilliant, colorful air current.

"...You?!" Iska yelled without thinking.

The malevolent angel Kelvina, who had fallen into the crushed furnace, crawled out, even after losing her wings.

However...

What Iska could scarcely believe he was seeing wasn't that his opponent had gotten back up.

"Your body..."

"What? None of this is unexpected."

As Kelvina crawled out of the furnace, he noticed that cracks had formed all over her transparent, gemlike form.

Despite the fact that she was a transcendental being, something impervious to many of the laws of physics, her body had begun to crumble in the stream of astral energy.

Like a sandcastle being blown away with the wind.

"That element within malevolent angels and witches cannot coexist with this planet's astral power. It's like water and fire. So when it is exposed to a large amount of astral energy...this is the result. My body is rejecting it..."

"..."

"Astral energy doesn't have adverse effects on humans, but it's like poison to me."

Fwoom...

The furnace that had been creating tremors stopped as abruptly as a string being cut. The once-human woman shrugged, looking on as though she was amused.

"This is why I took care not to damage the furnaces, at least. Well, you put up a good fight. I can't believe you'd drop me into one of these, of all things."

"...Well..."

Iska hadn't been trying to do that. He had just meant to get her to the golem. That was all he'd been trying to do.

"It was a coincidence."

"...I detest that word more than any other. Not only is it unscientific and dependent on outside factors, it has no elegance."

The corners of the mad scientist's lips curled. She seemed rather amused.

"At the very least, I think you should have said the same thing Elletear would have. *This is the will of the planet.* How about something poetic like that?"

"...Elletear."

"I hate the word *coincidence*, but the planet does indeed have a will. As you can see."

As her body crumbled away like sand, the malevolent angel Kelvina craned her neck upward; that was the only part she could still move. She gazed at the stream of eddying lights.

Red, blue, green, white, and yellow.

The astral energy that glittered like a mirage was swirling. Though the mad scientist had called it "a poison," the sight seemed to comfort her.

"'I hear the song of the astral powers. A divine tune conferred by ten billion stars.'"

"What?"

"That was what she told me. That she'd gained the ability to hear it. I wasn't able to make it out, but I thought if I could just reach the planet's core, that even I—that was what I'd believed, at least..."

She exhaled a long, deep breath. The vestiges of when she had once been human.

"Hey, Nazariel. I wasn't able to reach the planet's core...the city of ten billion stars, Leinenheib. But if this is also part of the grand will, then so be it."

"Uh?! Wait, Kelvina!"

"If the whims of the planet allow it, I hope we will meet again."

There was a roar.

The angel's crumbling body was engulfed in violet astral flames. It happened so suddenly, Iska didn't have time to yell.

"For I am a grotesque moth. I will never be compatible with a beautiful butterfly."

The mad scientist who had come into contact with the taboo disappeared into the glow of the blaze.

CHAPTER 7

Above Heaven, Below Heaven, Precious Only to Us

1

More than three miles underground. The Imperial capital.

It could be reached only through a gigantic elevator set up within the central base of the Imperial capital, which led to the greatest authoritative body in the Empire—the Imperial assembly.

It was nearly closing time.

The hall filled with hundreds of lawmakers was currently dead silent. With the exception of the eight people leading the assembly, that was.

"The signal from Kelvina has ceased transmission."

"And the witch princess Sisbell has escaped. So we have lost a precious purebred. Moreover, the pets and research documents caught up in the astral energy surge were also lost…"

One dejected sigh after another emitted from the monitors along the wall. Sighs that the Eight Great Apostles hadn't experienced in a hundred years.

"The Successor of the Black Steel. I suppose we've given him too much freedom."

"He's Crossweil's pupil. I didn't think we would be able to control him easily, but he has certainly exceeded our calculations."

"Yes. We should have simply commanded him to capture the Ice Calamity Witch and been done with it."

The witch jailbreak incident from a year ago.

It had all started when they had believed they could use the former Saint Disciple Iska, who had still been serving a sentence.

"We shall have you do something you ought to do."

"Capture the Ice Calamity Witch."

Why had they asked him to arrest her?

They hadn't intended to use her as a hostage. It hadn't been to eliminate a threat to the Imperial forces. They had done it because they needed her for one of Kelvina's experiments.

"The eldest daughter was too dangerous to use as a subject. We had the third daughter in prison a year ago..."

"Had we been able to capture the purebred second daughter, Aliceliese, instead, we would have had no qualms using her as a new subject, however..."

If that had gone differently...

Had Iska won in his first battle against the Ice Calamity Witch in the Nelka forest, they would have been able to send her to the Birthplace of Witches as a new subject.

"The Successor of the Black Steel knows too much."

"What shall we do about the other three members of Unit 907?"

"Eliminating him alone should suffice. If the entire unit disappears, even the Imperial headquarters might begin to act."

"Then we should move quickly. Before the Lord notices."

Applause rang out.

As the assembly hall went silent, a new proposal had been approved of without the knowledge of any other assembly members.

"We will execute former Saint Disciple Iska."

2

Birthplace of Witches.

Sisbell's eyes glittered as the pair emerged from the door of the astral power institute.

"Iska! And Rin! You're both safe!"

"It was really close, though. I have no idea what would have happened if Rin hadn't been there."

"...Same goes for you."

Rin stood up as Iska let her down.

She was pouting and seemed rather cross.

"I can't believe you practically came out unscathed while I was the only one who suffered blows... Ouch."

"Rin?!"

"...No, I apologize, Lady Sisbell. There is nothing wrong with me at all."

"But you look like you're in terrible pain."

"I will treat myself later."

Rin straightened herself before Sisbell. The left side of her face was blue and swollen, and her clothes had been sliced from her shoulder down her side. It was easy to see she was hurting.

"We're also glad that you're all safe," Iska said.

"No, I'm happy you're safe, Iska. All we did was run... Oh, but there was that weird ghostlike thing that caught us on the way out, though."

"We'll swap stories later. Let's get out of here."

Jhin heaved his gun case onto his shoulder and motioned with just his eyes to the roof of the ruins.

There were holes of various sizes, left in the wake of the astral energy that had surged up from underground.

"Given all the astral light that shot up, there are gonna be one or two witnesses outside. If they catch sight of us, they'll think we're suspicious. We need to book it, at least to beyond the wall."

"W-wait! We're doing more running?!"

Jhin, the commander, and Nene had started sprinting as fast as they could go. Sisbell also tried to race as fast as she could so she wouldn't be left behind. But the moment she lifted her leg to make a break for it...

...a thin strand of light appeared out of the blue.

It was finer than a hair. The glowing string, which seemed thin enough to melt into the atmosphere, shot toward Sisbell's neck as though lunging for prey.

The princess herself hadn't realized she was being targeted.

Iska, who had been watching his own companions, had been slightly too slow.

Only one person was able to react.

That one person was a certain Sovereignty servant whose eyes had never left Sisbell.

"Lady Sisbell!"

"What?! ......Rin?!"

The princess screamed.

Rin, who leaped on her, was caught in the strand of light that had appeared from nowhere. It was like a thread from a spiderweb. As it bound Rin's arms and legs, several more strings appeared to immobilize her.

"What?!"

"What...? Miss Rin?! That's!"

Jhin, Nene, and Commander Mismis noticed the situation behind them. Before the three of them could act, Iska had unsheathed his black astral sword.

"Rin, don't move! I'll—"

"All right, Isk. You're the one who shouldn't move, got that?"

His feet locked into place, as though he were frozen.

It's not that he had obeyed the command. Rather, he had stopped in his tracks from the surprise of a door opening out of thin air and the unexpected person who had appeared from it.

"...Why...?"

"Hmm? Why what, Isk?"

"...Why...are you here?"

From below black-rimmed glasses, the clever-looking officer of the Imperial forces smiled mischievously.

Risya In Empire.

The Saint Disciple of the fifth seat and the Lord's staff officer.

"Risya?!"

"Yoo-hoo, Mismis. It's been a while. How have you been?"

Risya gave Mismis, whose voice cracked from surprise, an off-handed wave. She used her other hand to reel in Rin, who had been caught in astral threads.

"R-Risya, that light isn't..."

"Oh, you mean this? That's right—it's astral power. But make sure you keep it a secret from the other Imperial force members."

"What?!"

"Also, Isk."

The Saint Disciple had once again turned her gaze on him, her perceptive eyes already locked onto the black sword he held at the ready.

"How long are you going to keep that out? Sheathe that blade, will you?"

"............"

"Oh, what's wrong?"

"...I will. But please explain what's happening."

He returned the weapon to its sheath. Rin was still bound and immobilized. Behind him, he could feel Sisbell glued to his back, shaking uncontrollably.

...I don't know what happened, but this is bad.

...Unit 907 has been spotted with two witches.

And by a Saint Disciple at that.

It was treason. They'd likely be executed. Rin and Sisbell as well. That, or they might even face a fate worse than death.

"I'm going to be frank. Are you going to put us down?"

"What a good question, Isk. So you know exactly where you stand. It seems you haven't completely abandoned your duty as an Imperial soldier."

"............"

"So I'll answer you. Isk, this is the Empire. I don't have the power to decide that. Whether an Imperial soldier lives or dies—"

Risya looked up at the sky.

Another door of light opened above her head.

"—can only be decided by Lord Yunmelngen."

A silver-haired beast leaped from the door of light. Somersaulting around like a cat, they landed lightly next to Risya.

"Was that a good introduction, Your Excellency?"

"You may do as you like. I don't have any interest in how you introduce me."

The beast stood on two legs.

"Th-they talk?!"

"Did you think only humans were capable of speech? ...Oh. I suppose phrasing it that way will cause misunderstandings. Well, I suppose I don't mind that."

The beast smiled at Mismis. Though they had the splendid fur of a fox, their face was between that of a human and a cat. And while their eyes held the charm of a child, they were also strangely uncanny.

A fox? A cat?

What kind of beast was this?

"...Hey, Miss Saint Disciple." Jhin, very deliberately, looked between Risya and the beast next to her. "Knock it off with the jokes."

"Hmm? What's the joke, Jhin-Jhin?"

"His Excellency is a hulking man with a beard. He comes by once a year to the Imperial base."

"Yes, he's a body double. The ninth one, historically, in fact."

"......What did you say?" Jhin was taken aback. "What does that mean? You're saying he's a fake?!"

"That's right. I mean, look how tiny the actual Lord is. The civilians would raise a stink if they found out." Risya easily nodded. "The real Lord is standing next to me."

"..."

"Oh, you still don't believe me?"

"...Course not." Jhin accepted her gaze fully as he said that. "That talking animal surprised me, but what you're saying is impossible... We didn't join the Imperial forces to serve some creature."

"In that case, why do you think you joined?" the silver-haired beast asked. There was intelligence in their eyes. And a glint of fangs in their mouth. **"If you think that a staff officer and Saint Disciple serve someone other than the Lord Yunmelngen, please enlighten me as to who it could be."**

"......Uh."

"So you may think of this as an honor. I rarely show myself, after all."

None of them had anything to say. Even Rin, who was struggling against the astral threads she was caught in, was appalled and distracted as she listened to the beast. Iska couldn't stop his legs from shivering in place.

...Is this beast supposed to be the Lord?

...Ridiculous. How could anyone ask us to believe that?!

His rational mind refused to let him accept it.

However, there was something peculiar about the beast's aura, something uncannily intimidating. Though they weren't going to fight, Iska felt something radiating off the creature that was even greater than the aura of a purebred. It was almost like that of the Founder.

"Ah, so you're Iska."

A smile reached the Lord's eyes, which narrowed into the shape of crescent moons.

"You're Crossweil's successor, yes? You have the astral swords, so you must be."

"...Why do you know my master?!"

"I know him better than you do. Yes, I came to chat."

Pat.

The beast placed a hand on Rin's head.

"Why, you little!"

"Oh, what a feisty witch you are. I haven't had a human try to bite me in a while. Seems you'll be entertaining. Well, I am pleased with this. Let us go home, Risya."

"What? Already? Weren't we going to check out this facility?"

"The ninth seat can do that. My priority is playing with this witch. See."

The Lord grabbed Rin's neck. The moment they did that, they finally turned their gaze ahead.

"Third Princess Sisbell."

"H-how do you know who I am?!"

"Let us have a conversation in the Imperial capital. This also concerns you."

Then they disappeared...

...through the door of light, with Risya and Rin behind them.

"I will be waiting, Successor of the Black Steel. Let us speak of matters that will determine the planet's fate."

EPILOGUE

The Land Where It Started

1

Several days earlier.

One of the two world superpowers.

In the center of the Nebulis Sovereignty, also known as the Paradise of Witches, were several globally renowned research institutes that excelled in astral power engineering.

The Hydra's scientific institute and astral power engineering research center: Snow and Sun.

A facility run by one of the three royal families.

They had created this laboratory to investigate methods of sparking a fourth energy revolution through using the astral energy that surged from the planet's core in place of electricity and gas.

A copse of trees a few hundred yards from the establishment.

"Mizerhyby Hydra Nebulis IX…I see. Obviously the head of house would leave Snow and Sun in your hands. Your astral power is glorious, well suited for a purebred."

The handsome white-haired man roughly pushed back his bangs.

He had commanding eyebrows and a deep-set face. His self-confidence, appearance, manly allure, and comportment made him seem the spitting image of a first-class stage actor.

And that man was...

"How long do you plan on sleeping?" he asked in a voice tinged with exasperation as he addressed the older gentleman on the ground. "Shuvalts, you think you're allowed to act senile after taking charge of Mira's education?"

"...I am not Her Majesty's... Right now...I am her daughter's servant."

He staggered to his feet. His eyes were deeply sunken, as were his cheeks. But of course he would look like that. He had been abducted by the Hydra and imprisoned for quite a while in the basement of Snow and Sun.

This was the third princess's attendant, Shuvalts.

The fact that he could still stand up through sheer force of will despite being so exhausted was what made him Sisbell's one and only attendant.

"......Salinger. It's been thirty long years...you villain."

He steadied himself on the trunk of a tree. He was out of breath, but his eyes showed no hesitation as he glared at the sorcerer.

"You...freed me..."

"Just to pester them," the man feared as the transcendental sorcerer answered with a straight face. "I wanted to give the Hydra a little trouble. I don't care why you were trapped in Snow and Sun, but I'm sure losing their captive will hurt."

That would likely distract the Hydra.

It had been a trivial decision.

"............"

"What? If you can glare at me, then you should get going to

the palace quick as you can. The Hydra assassins will come to prowl these woods soon."

"Salinger, you…"

The elderly man's shoulders sagged as he breathed. Once he'd served as Queen Mirabella's teacher; now he was Princess Sisbell's attendant.

"You think I would forget? You tried attacking Her Majesty on countless occasions."

"You're right."

"…So did you break out to make another attempt on her life?"

"What? Has your senility reached your brain?" The white-haired, brawny man gave a large sigh. "Why do you assume I would be fixated on her? How paltry. How about you stop babbling that nonsense and tell me something useful?"

"Huh?"

"What are the Hydra planning?" The sorcerer stared into the attendant's eyes. "I wanted the secret Princess Mizerhyby was put in charge of, but unfortunately, I never found it. But you must have heard something about it, seeing as you were her hostage."

"…I regret to inform you that I only learned a single piece of information."

"Well, out with it."

"The Hydra are colluding with the Empire. Either by sharing military forces or astral power research. Possibly both."

"What?"

The white-haired Adonis went silent. Folding his arms, he looked away from the older man almost as though he had lost interest and stared into the air. He scowled.

"Odd. I doubt the Imperial forces would join hands with the Hydra to that extent. In which case…"

He turned his back on the elderly man and started walking.

"So it's Yunmelngen. Or perhaps there are still others in the Empire."

2

Imperial territory. Easternmost Altoria jurisdiction.

Birthplace of Witches.

"...I'm going to the Imperial capital!" Sisbell's voice broke the silence that had hung over them like a dark cloud. It was almost as though she was attempting to motivate herself. "I can't face Alice if I return to the Sovereignty but sacrifice Rin in the process. So I must return to the Imperial capital and bring her back!"

"By yourself?"

"With the help of you all, of course!"

"...You sure don't have any qualms about roping us into this mess." Jhin let out a sigh he had been holding in. He met the girl's stern gaze as he spoke, seeming somewhat resigned. "Their Excellency summoned us there themself. If we don't go, we'll all end up being wanted for treason...and if we do that obediently, they'll imprison us."

"So about that..." Iska reluctantly followed up Jhin. "I've been prepared for this from the start. I was thinking we might all end up executed."

Rin and Sisbell were both witches. Unit 907 had invited both of them into the Empire, but now the Lord and their staff officer had found out.

...And they've asked us to come to the capital.

...That's basically the same thing as telling us to give up and accept our deaths. That's got to be what they're thinking.

But the more time passed, the more Iska's thoughts on the matter started to change.

"I know this is just me trying to be optimistic, but..."

"Well, out with it."

"We can flee the Empire right away. Basically, I think the Lord might not have considered we'd defect. We could go to a neutral city or anywhere, really."

They had Princess Sisbell in tow. At the moment, it was possible for them to defect to the Sovereignty.

"The Lord purposefully abandoned us and disappeared. If they actually wanted to execute us, wouldn't they have sent the Imperial forces after us?"

"............" Jhin scowled.

"What if they're not planning on putting us to death and actually meant they want us to go back to the capital exactly like they said?"

"...I—I think they do, too!" Commander Mismis, who had been quiet until then, shot her hand up. "I have no idea what the Lord could be thinking, but something's been bugging me."

"What's that?"

"Risya's face." There was something firm in the commander's expression as she said that—something like conviction. "I don't think she looked that angry... I mean, think about it. Risya has even more ties to the Sovereignty than we do—she was actually using astral power! It's an even playing field!"

"But there's still a chance they're trying to silence us at the last minute."

"...That's true, but that's not what it seemed from the look on Risya's face!" Commander Mismis turned. She looked at Nene and nodded as though urging her. "What do you think, Nene?"

"...I think I'll do whatever everyone else does, whether that's defecting or going to the capital. But if we do switch sides, I think my parents would worry." Nene let out a heavy sigh. "And I'm only saying this now, but I think I'm still feeling shaken from seeing the Lord like that."

"R-right, Nene!" Mismis added. "I was also bewildered... Iska, didn't you meet the Lord when you became a Saint Disciple?"

"I didn't see their face. There was a thin curtain between us when I had an audience with them."

Iska didn't have an answer. He might have been more shocked than anyone else, in fact.

…The Saint Disciples exist in order to serve the Lord as soldiers.

…I can't believe I was risking my life to protect a monster like that.

And the same held true for the astral power research the Empire had been conducting. His love and trust in his homeland seemed close to crumbling into nothing.

"No, actually, I can see this happening. If that's Lord Yunmelngen."

"Huh?"

They all turned. They looked at Sisbell, who seemed resolved.

"Please remember Kelvina from just earlier, everyone. She said that she was the one who made Vichyssoise like that. And you saw with your own eyes how she turned into a monster."

"…Miss Sisbell," Nene said hesitantly. "Are you saying that the Lord is like her? You think it's possible being exposed to astral energy transformed them into that?"

"Well, think about it." Sisbell turned around. She looked far into the distant western sky.

"The first place in the world where astral power erupted was the Empire."

A century ago…

The discovery of the world's first vortex served as the origin of all witches and sorcerers. It had also resulted in the birth of the Founder, Nebulis.

"But what if the Revered Founder wasn't the only one? What if Lord Yunmelngen was also showered in astral energy a hundred years ago?"

That would explain their physical appearance. And that would also shine a light on Kelvina's research—perhaps they were creating a second or third Lord, or they were trying to find a way to return the Lord to their original form.

"Iska, this also concerns us."

"What?"

"The reason why I came to this assumption right away and why I snuck into the Empire a year ago was to research this."

"...What did you just say?"

"I simply was curious. I didn't intend to do anything to the Empire. I just wanted to know the truth of what happened a century ago."

It all started in the capital one hundred years prior. Witches and sorcerers had been created, and the Nebulis Sovereignty had spawned from the supernation that had been the Empire at the time. Everything that had happened until now traced its origins to that place.

"I was set back from going through with my plan at the time. Immediately after setting foot in the Empire, I was arrested and imprisoned. And you saved me after that, Iska, but...but I think now I can do it. No, there's no other time to do it but now!"

She shook her brilliant hair and tightened her expression.

Sisbell Lou Nebulis IX. The witch who possessed the Illumination astral power that could see the past placed her hand to her chest.

"The events that took place a century ago. I don't imagine that the surge of astral energy in the capital could have simply been a coincidence, of all things. But why did it happen in the Imperial capital? I am sure that place holds other secrets."

If they went to the capital...

As long as they had Sisbell's astral power, they would be able to re-create a scene of what had transpired a century ago.

"So, just as I asked you from the start, I want to travel to the capital. We were invited there by the Lord themself, after all."

She kept her hand to her chest. The Nebulis Sovereignty princess almost seemed to sing as she declared...

"First, we shall save Rin. And then we shall uncover the world's oldest mystery."

Afterword

None but the Lord stands at the pinnacle of the world.

Thank you for picking up the ninth volume of *Our Last Crusade or the Rise of a New World* (*Last Crusade*).

This volume's theme was "inhuman."

In this world, where people fear witches and sorcerers for the astral power dwelling within them, the truly inhuman actors who had been manipulating the course of history finally make an appearance.

In the Sovereignty, the Zoa and Hydra are honing their claws.

In the Empire, powerful people begin to clash.

The curtain has risen on the symbol of a new era, the Imperial Taboo Saga!

On the other hand...

This ninth volume has Rin sightseeing (?) in the Empire and, after this and that, she ends up making Alice upset by getting too close to Iska. On top of that, the queen discovers Alice's precious video (which Alice made sure to get back). I think that the eighth volume had a lot more going on than the seventh.

And then there's Sisbell!

Alice prepares as much as she can to present a united front with the little sister she is frightened of in many ways.

Meanwhile, in the Imperial capital, which will serve as the next stage, the bigwigs have gathered in full force. Of course, Alice will have her time to shine even though she was left in the Sovereignty, so I hope you have high expectations for the next volume as well!

Well then, that's it for the story in this volume, so I'll move on to announcements.

In the eighth volume, I announced that *Last Crusade* had been greenlit for an anime. Since then and up to the ninth volume, we've been making arrangements for it. I've been allowed to participate in the script meetings, and I've also had the opportunity to see the character sheets as they've been finishing them up! They're all wonderful, and I look forward every day to seeing the anime take shape.

I'm sure there are many people who are interested to know who the voice actors for Iska and Alice will be, so I hope you'll enjoy them being announced after this!

Now I need to talk about my concurrent series.

My MF Bunko J series has also reached its climax, so I would be so happy if you would support it as well.

▾*Why Does No One Remember My World?*

The eighth volume in the series has been published. The manga version is serialized in *Monthly Comic Alive*, and it's doing so well, there are even plans for a French version to be published.

I haven't had my previous series released in France before, so I'm glad to have this opportunity for my story to spread further.

(Please take a look at the Japanese versions of Volumes 1 through 5 of the manga as well!)

▾Announcement about *Last Crusade*'s short stories!

Now for an announcement about the next volume.

We're finally rushing right into the Empire arc and the pandemoniac tenth volume…but before that, I have a great announcement.

At present, Fantasia Bunko's *Dragon Magazine* is publishing bimonthly installments of *Last Crusade* short stories, which are set to be released as a collection!

After receiving requests for a short story collection from so many, it's finally come to fruition!

The Empire and the Sovereignty.

As the two superpowers wage war, these tales delve into the background of the *Last Crusade* saga, into Iska's everyday life in the capital and Alice's days in the palace.

▾*Our Last Crusade or the Rise of a New World: Secret File (Last Crusade: Secret File)*.

Coming to you this summer!

I'm planning to pen an exclusive story and epilogue worthy of being labeled "top secret" to accompany the stories published by *Dragon Magazine*. I hope you'll enjoy it!

And so the afterword has come to an end.

Many people helped me with the ninth volume as well.

My editor Y.

You had the most daily involvement in *Last Crusade*'s manuscript and writing process. As we steadily work to prepare for the anime, I'm looking forward to continuing to work with you!

To the illustrator, Ao Nekonabe.

Thank you so much for the incredibly cool Rin on the cover!

I feel like Rin, who has often been in a supporting role until now, has finally become the center of both the book's content and illustrations in this ninth volume.

Also, I'd actually really like to write here the names of all the people working on the anime...but I'll let you enjoy that later.

Well then...

The next volume of *Our Last Crusade or the Rise of a New World* will be the short story collection.

A tale of the swordsman Iska and the witch princess Alice.

I hope you'll enjoy these glimpses into their lives as war rages between their two countries.

Well then, I hope we'll meet again in the summer for *Last Crusade: Secret File* (short story collection).

On an afternoon in spring,

Kei Sazane

Announcement:
VOLUME 10

How about a tale from the old days?
This one is from a time when the Founder was still a young girl living in the Empire.

Lord Yunmelngen abruptly makes an appearance, beckoning Iska and the others to the Imperial capital.
They journey there to save Rin and learn the truth of a hundred years ago.
As though in concert with them, Alice has taken up the role of the queen's proxy in the Sovereignty and is forced to make a shocking choice.

The tenth act of the Grand Witch and the most powerful swordsman's dance.
The planet's ancient taboo awakens from its century-long slumber.

Short Story Collection:

Our Last Crusade or the Rise of a New World: Secret File

COMING SOON!

Our Last CRUSADE OR THE RISE OF A New World

VOLUME 10
Coming soon

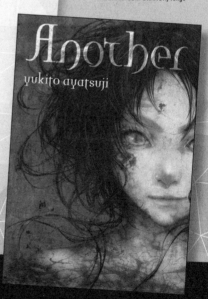

The Detective Is Already Dead

When the story begins without its hero

Kimihiko Kimizuka has always been a magnet for trouble and intrigue. For as long as he can remember, he's been stumbling across murder scenes or receiving mysterious attaché cases to transport. When he met Siesta, a brilliant detective fighting a secret war against an organization of pseudohumans, he couldn't resist the call to become her assistant and join her on an epic journey across the world.

...Until a year ago, that is. Now he's returned to a relatively normal and tepid life, knowing the adventure must be over. After all, the detective is already dead.

Volume 1 available wherever books are sold!

YenPress.com

TANTEI HA MO, SHINDEIRU. Vol. 1
©nigozyu 2019
Illustration: Umibouzu
KADOKAWA CORPORATION